Center for Basque Studies
Basque Literature Series, No. 5

BASQUE LITERATURE SERIES

ARANTXA URRETABIZKAIA

The Red Notebook

Translated from Basque by
Kristin Addis

Basque Literature Series Editor
Mari Jose Olaziregi

Center for Basque Studies
University of Nevada, Reno

Center for Basque Studies
Basque Literature Series, No. 5

Center for Basque Studies
University of Nevada, Reno
Reno, Nevada 89557
http://basque.unr.edu

Basque Literature Series Editor: Mari Jose Olaziregi

Series design © 2008 by Jose Luis Agote.
Cover design by Jose Luis Agote.

Library of Congress Cataloging-in-Publication Data

Urretavizcaya, Arantxa.
 [Koaderno gorria. English]
 The red notebook / by Arantxa Urretabizkaia; translated from
Basque by Kristin Addis.
   p. cm. -- (Basque literature series ; no. 5)
 Summary: "The Red Notebook belongs to the autobiographical
genre and the novel-writing tradition that deals with the female
voice and memory. This novel breaks new ground from a physical
and psychological point of view, bringing out the social and
political aspects of motherhood"--Provided by publisher.
 ISBN 978-1-877802-82-9 (pbk.)
 I. Addis, Kristin. II. Title. III. Series.

 PH5339.U645K6313 2008
 899'.923--dc22

2008045114

Acknowledgments

The Center for Basque Studies wishes to gratefully acknowledge the generous financial support of the Government of the Basque Autonomous Community for the publication of this book.

ONE

A young woman arrives at the Caracas airport. She flew alone and carries a bag in her hand. While she waits for her suitcases she does not set the bag down on the floor, even though it is quite heavy. At the woman's side, a small cart, empty.

When the first suitcases begin to go around on the carousel, she hangs the bag over her shoulder, strap across her chest, because she wants to have her hands free. One by one, the people around her pick up their luggage and head for the door without looking back. The woman is completely alone when the carousel stops going around. Mouth open, she looks around, bag dangling and the little cart at her side as empty as it was at the beginning. Worried, the woman asks at two or three windows, fills out the forms they offer her. They show her a dozen or so lost suitcases, but none is hers.

Finally, she has to leave for Caracas almost empty-handed, clutching the bag she has carried since the beginning tight to her body as if the world were full of thieves. She takes a taxi, despite having been advised beforehand not to, and gives the name of a hotel to the driver. On the way, her eyes close and she hardly looks out the window. She knows the city is far away and she is anxious to reach the hotel since she feels that she won't be able to relax until she locks the door of her room behind her. At first, the driver asks where she's from and whether she'll be staying for very long in Caracas, but soon he is also quiet, silenced by her brusque answers.

They arrive at the main entrance to the hotel in silence and the woman pays the fare without haggling. With no luggage, she moves quickly and is immediately in the lobby. In front of her, between the door and the reception desk, a young man holds a heavy weapon against his chest, eyes alert and body as straight as if he were made of stone.

As soon as she enters her room, she locks the door and lies down on the bed, still holding onto her bag. After a few seconds, she sits up, removes the strap of the bag from around her neck and examines the room without much interest. She turns on the air conditioning, takes off her shoes and then, only then, does she open the bag.

Clumsy with fatigue and the hassle with the suitcase, she takes out a package, removes the string and the paper, and places the contents on the table on the left side of the room: a red notebook, a photograph, and a small piece of paper with something written on it. The picture is in color and shows a little girl holding a boy by the arm. They are looking at each other, and the girl's face has a soft smile, noticeable more in her eyes than on her lips. The boy's face can't be seen very well because he is half turned away from the camera.

For a few long seconds, the woman stands still, look-ing at what she took out of the package. She puts down the photo and touches the notebook, but does not open it. After backing up a couple of steps, she sniffs her armpits with a sigh. She takes her toiletries kit out of her bag and goes into the bathroom.

Before showering, she washes the jacket she was wear-ing in the sink with hand soap. She spreads it out flat on a towel and gets under the shower as if she were jumping into a swimming pool.

"I am your mother. I gave birth to you, Miren, and you, Beñat, thirteen and ten years ago. Seven years ago, you disappeared, stolen from me by your father. That is my truth, that and the fact that I don't know what your father has told you about me.

"I have been looking for you these seven years, and a few months ago I managed to find out that you are in Caracas.

"This is the beginning, my darlings, and it doesn't seem too bad for a sad story that might have a happy ending.

"Right now, as soon as I got this notebook, on the 5th of October, 1990, I begin what I have owed you for so long. In fact, it's your birthday, Beñat. Happy birthday, sweetheart, I wish you happiness forever.

"This is certainly not the first time I've tried to do this. Before this, I wrote a draft, even though people in my situation may not write what they want. At that time, though, I didn't know what I know now.

"During these long years, I have told you every night what happened in the day; the journal I never wrote for reasons of security is for you. I still know some parts of it by heart: without exaggerating, almost all of what I have written up to now and what is yet to come. So I don't have to think as I go on; my hand writes automatically, obeying a silent dictaphone, as if it had been created for just that purpose.

"I don't know for sure if you are still in Caracas, much less how you live, what you hope for from life, how you see the world, how you ease your pain, your sadness, your doubts, what you hold onto as you fall asleep at night to keep the nightmares away.

"I know only one thing for sure, and it is enough to make me write this lengthy work: if you call the woman who lives with you *mamá*, it is because your memory of me has been stolen from you, and with it your childhood and maybe even the Basque language itself.

"Seven long years have passed since the last time we saw each other. You were six years old, Miren, and you, Beñat, were three. It was in the French Basque Country, in the summer, and that day I would never have guessed what would come later. A mother hugs her children under the summer sun; it's insignificant, something that happens a million times a day.

"Nevertheless, I remember everything that happened that morning, and I have often gone back over it, as if it were a videotape, forward, rewind, fast, slow. The sun barely pierced the pine forest, as if it didn't care what was happening on the grass below. You, little Miren, had your head in my lap; you were attentive, watching me without question. I haven't forgotten, nor will I ever forget, what a terrible cry you made, Beñat, when you had to leave. Those cries have been, ever after, the music of most of my nightmares, a refrain that heralds nothing good.

"So it was that you soon disappeared completely and I lost track of you. I managed to find out that you didn't live in our house any more and that they knew nothing of you at your school. I cast my net wider and caught nothing: your grandmother also claimed to know nothing of you. Looking at a small atlas then without knowing where to rest my eyes, I saw how big this planet is, this small piece of rock in the universe. I thought you were lost forever; I learned what true fear is, emptiness, isolation.

"But the harm your father has done me was nothing compared to what he did to you. That's why I started writing this, to protect your rights, not mine."

TWO

The woman who lost her suitcase at the airport is sitting at the table in the hotel room, wearing the jacket she washed by hand the night before. The wide black skirt she wore with it is on the bed. She is writing, quickly, as if she were taking down on paper what someone else is saying.

"I found them, that's the first thing I have to tell you. I arrived here yesterday and today, after lunch, I took the photo and went to the school. It was incredibly hot and I was still wearing the clothes I wore for the journey. They lost my suitcase at the airport and haven't found it yet. I was carrying what you gave me in my handbag, of course.

"The heat was suffocating, but you don't want to hear about that now, or about my suitcase. I got to the school and sat down on a bench in front of it, sweating like a pig, with the photo hidden in a book. All of a sudden, the children started coming out, most of them running without taking any notice of the furnace outside. I saw them immediately, holding each other by the arm just like in the picture, and looking at each other as if there were no one else around them.

"Let me say first of all that they are beautiful, slender without being fragile. The girl, in addition to looking incredibly like you, looks older than she is.

"As soon as they reached the school gate, they stopped, aimlessly, it seemed to me. The girl took the backpack the boy was carrying on his back and brushed his hair back from his face. The boy's hair is curly and rather long, quite a bit lighter than yours, but not blond.

"I left the bench and approached them. When I heard the girl's voice, I stopped to keep up appearances. She has a low voice, almost like a grown woman's. She was speaking in Spanish, but said *father* in Basque. In the two sentences I heard, she didn't mention the other woman. I went a little bit closer and just then an ancient van stopped in front of the children and the driver blew the horn. They both headed for it without rushing. The driver was a woman, with long, straight, black hair, a wide face, and slanted, tired eyes. In a word, she looked Indian. The children got in the van, into the back seat, and didn't kiss the woman. They started playing with a small child who was buckled into the back seat.

"I wrote down the license number and watched them drive away: the van plunged onto one of those highways that tangle up together in the city center. Even with the heat, I shivered. Then I came right back to the hotel to write this note, so that you would know I'm off to a good start."

The woman rereads what she has written, felt-tip pen between her lips. Then, she writes L at the bottom of the page, puts the paper in an envelope and stands up, looking at the clock. It is hot, even with the fan on. For a moment she doesn't know whether to go out with the envelope or not. She decides not to and returns to the table. She picks up the red notebook and begins to read, on the bed again. The sky outside begins to go red, but she doesn't turn on the light.

"You disappeared then, completely, and for nearly seven years I had no news of you. In that terrible period, I asked myself over and over if you had really been born or if you were merely a figment of my anguished imagination.

"And suddenly, at the beginning of this year, I found out through your grandmother that you were living in Venezuela, and that your father had married again there and had had a third child. This news, of course, did not come to me directly but arrived second- or third-hand. Last Christmas, you apparently wrote to your grandmother and didn't mention me at all.

"I must say that it was hard for me to believe what I heard; I hadn't expected that from your father. How the hell can someone marry if he's still married? I didn't recognize in your father this reported desire for affairs, nor his hatred of me. In the years we were together, it was he who balanced my ambition; he was my angel until you, Miren, were born.

"The news was hard for me to believe, but I had to hear it. Besides, Venezuela was not so foreign to me. I had an uncle there for many years, who had fled to Venezuela after we Basques had lost the war, and some of the fellow fighters who had worked with me for years were there too. I gave one of them the task of looking for you.

"I hope that you will soon understand, but let me say right now, I couldn't go looking for you, I couldn't tell you where I was. Moreover, I didn't know myself exactly where I was, just as I don't know tonight either. I can tell you what I see from the window and it's not much: two beech trees that are not yet showing the first signs of fall, the stars that keep me company in my bed at night, a lonely bird that calls sadly once in a while.

"So I gave the task to a friend, and yesterday, after six months, that friend got a photo to me. You mustn't think it was easy for him; there was no trace of you at the Basque Center or at the Consulate. He had to go from school to school, but that was the least of it.

"I have a photo of you, which is now on the table leaning against the wall, you two holding each other by the arm, looking at each other, just the two of you, though you can tell there are lots of other kids around. I know it by heart already, and it seems to me that the way you look today is closer to how you will look as adults than the way you looked before. Your hair has gotten darker, Miren, and yours, Beñat, has gone curly. That's what was the hardest for me to grasp, because you're the image of your father, Beñat, not like you were when you were little, and it unnerved me completely to see the face of one I loved so much at one time.

"Together with the photo there was a brief report, just a short one, half a dozen lines. You are living in Caracas, you go to school there and you are good students. The note said that your teachers think you have a good relationship with your parents. With your parents, they said, not with your father and stepmother. However, the woman who lives with you is not your mother but your stepmother, according to my dictionary."

L closes the notebook. While she was reading, the sky has gone from red to purple and then to dark blue. This is why she gives up reading: she no longer has enough light. Her eyes feel swollen and she has a lump in her throat. She stands up, but doesn't turn on the light. She takes a few steps without thinking about what she's doing. She needs to talk to someone, but she doesn't know anyone in Caracas. The sentences she just read are bouncing around inside her head, and her thoughts turn to the person who wrote them.

Find them, she remembers, speak to them and then you decide whether or not to give them the notebook. Find them and love them, as much as you can, if only for a moment.

L shakes her head because she doesn't want to cry. Then her mood shifts like mist dispelled by the wind. She turns on the light and makes a phone call. She wants to rent a car the next day and she's having trouble deciding what car would be best. She doesn't want an automatic— those are for people who can't drive—and she doesn't want one of those huge things that have taken over the city. She asks for a small Opel finally, neither red nor yellow.

After hanging up the phone, she places her right hand on the notebook but does not pick it up again. Instead, she opens her map of Caracas on the bed and traces the route from the hotel to the children's school again and again with her index finger, reading the names of the streets and avenues until she's sure she has them memorized.

This chant will be her only company while she leaves the hotel and eats dinner in the Chinese restaurant across the street. When she notices that she is drawing the route to the school with grains of rice, she decides to go for a short walk around the neighborhood, still unfamiliar to her, before returning to the hotel. It must be around ten o'clock at night and she doesn't see many people on the street. There are a few men and fewer women, all dressed well and fully made-up, as if instead of going home they

were all—young and old—on their way to an elegant
party.

The next day, early in the morning, L calls the airport. No, the damned suitcase has not turned up yet, but
she shouldn't give up. So she goes to a store next door to
the Chinese restaurant and there, among colorful, flam-
boyant dresses, finds some white pants and a black shirt
to buy, both of which are completely skin tight. The clerk
doesn't understand when she says they're a bit too reveal-
ing and praises no end her customer's slimness, her slender waist. She leaves the shop wearing the clothes, and she
thinks at once that her purchase was not really suitable;
the white pants will get dirty immediately. Nevertheless,
she is happy with the reflection she sees in the mirror.
Besides, like every time she's had to pay for something
since she came to Caracas, the clothes seemed cheap, even
though she has no extra money beyond what she will need
for the three weeks she will spend there.

When they tell her the car she rented is waiting for
her, she goes down to the lobby, dressed in black and
white and with her hair pulled back. The Opel is grey,
the color of dirty silver, and she drives without embarrassment among the much bigger cars. When she stops
at the first stoplight, L jumps: she thinks she sees Mother
just in front of the car, six feet away. But no, she realizes
immediately that it isn't. The woman walking to the left
in front of her is the same height, but doesn't look like
her. Nevertheless, her heart is still pounding as she puts
the Opel in gear again.

While she is still near the hotel, she leaves the Opel
parked badly and mails the letter she wrote the night
before. Before she puts the envelope into the mailbox, she

thinks perhaps the tone she adopted was too warm, or too cold.

Half an hour later, and without losing her way, L is waiting outside the school with the window rolled all the way down, thankful for the slightest breath of air. She doesn't have to wait long or at least it doesn't seem long to her. Almost as soon as the children begin to come out, she spots the girl and the boy and immediately starts the car. They are not arm-in-arm, but the girl still carries the boy's backpack.

The old van also arrives, earlier than the day before, with a man driving it and no child in the back. The children kiss the man as soon as they get in the car, and that's all L sees. She positions the Opel behind the van and concentrates on the rear of the vehicle. Even driving, there is no coolness, but she is concentrating too hard on the rear of the old heap in front of her to worry about the weather.

The father and children go a long way through the enormous city L doesn't yet know. I should spend my mornings here, she thinks, as she is in danger of losing the van in the millionth tie-up on the highway. By then it seems to her that she has crossed three or four different cities. First, the Manhattan of the movies, chockablock with skyscrapers; then the highways with so many beggar children at the stoplights; and third, the neighborhoods, each one poorer as they rise up the side of the mountain. Finally, at the top of a short but steep hill, the van slows, turns right, and stops after going through a half-rusted gate, huffing and puffing like an old elephant. San Luis, says a sign on the entrance.

As soon as they park, the three in the van are lost from sight inside a tall tower, but a few seconds later, she again catches sight of the boy and the girl, without the backpack and with a small black dog leaping around them. The two sit facing each other on the grass, which is almost as dry as straw, leaning in close to talk.

L doesn't dare leave her car and, while she's trying to decide what to do, she sees the father again, leading a toddler by the hand. The man disappears, and the three children and the dog stay on the lawn in front of the building. The girl appears even older than she did the day before, perhaps because the first buds of breasts can be seen under the t-shirt she is wearing, or perhaps because, when she is taking care of the child in her arms, her gestures are those of a mother. It always startles L, this transformation that motherhood brings to women, and now she sees that it is not necessary to give birth for this metamorphosis to take place.

She spies on the group for about half an hour from inside the Opel. In the meantime, the sun has gone down behind the tower, and the air is full of the smell of a flower L doesn't recognize. It must be about seven o'clock when the children disappear indoors, the older two holding the little one by the hands.

After they go in, L gets out of the car and, approaching the sign that says San Luis, unexpectedly meets a darkskinned old woman. Excuse me, she says, she's lost, she doesn't know where she is. The woman says some long names and a few numbers. Without taking her eyes from the building for a second, L writes down what she heard and finally asks the woman how to get back to the city. But no, the old woman can't explain that; she has to go down the hill, that's all.

She gets lost a thousand times on her way back to the hotel, but she doesn't care. It pained her more when the beggar children approached the Opel at the stoplight in the middle of nowhere. She wasn't afraid, but she didn't give them anything, even though they kept calling to her until the light changed color. It occurs to her that if she keeps going from curve to curve she'll eventually end up in the Basque Country. But no. Just as the twilight becomes apparent over the Manhattan of skyscrapers, she sees the name of the hotel right in front of her.

The beggar children she saw on the highway are getting confused in her mind with the children at San Luis, but she doesn't forget her first accomplishment: day two and she knows where the children live. Encouraged by this happy thought, she doesn't feel the slightest trace of fear when she passes the armed man in the lobby.

No, they didn't call from the airport. She looks down and, yes, the once white pants are now grey from the pockets to the knees, but she doesn't care. Suddenly, she thinks that the clothes she brought are not at all appropriate; they are too different, too obviously chosen to hide the body she likes despite its faults. She is amazed at the thought, as if someone else had suggested that she should buy new clothes.

THREE

"Since then, I have read the report a million times, without doing anything else all evening but examine your photo, stroke it, trying to imagine your journey from the dusky pine grove in the French Basque Country to the door of that school in Caracas. It is you two, without a doubt, even though inside me, despite all my efforts, you have always been my three- and six-year-olds.

"I should say that my investigator didn't know that the children he was looking for were mine, because among us such details are not given. He followed his orders dutifully, blindly. The report that came with your photograph had the word *parent* in it, and that is what is nailed to my heart right now. I will thank him for his efforts, even if the most difficult thing still remains to be done.

"So I know where you are and with whom and, more or less, what you're up to. But the person who will get in touch with you, the one who will rebuild the broken bridge between us, needs different abilities, different eyes. The detective work is done, the foundation has been laid, but that's all.

"Let's say I'm blind and have to trust what someone else sees, or mute and must speak to you with someone else's tongue. That's our point of departure. I rapidly chose the eyes and tongue I needed from the limited possibilities around me. A friend, one whom I met after you disappeared, a lawyer and an honest person. If she accepts my offer, she will give you what I'm writing now.

"And I am writing, endlessly, until the dawn takes me, almost without thinking what I'm doing. It seems to me that it is enough for me to open my heart, that something has sprung forth there that propels the hand that reaches out to you of its own accord, pouring forth like a stream that has finally found its way to the ocean.

"I'm sure I've said that in all these years, not a single day has passed that I haven't thought about you; you are inside me, in all hours dark and bright. But, I now realize, always with the same bodies and faces, even after learning that you are alive and living in Venezuela. Until your photo arrived. The photo brought my image of you up to date, and what happened in that pine grove suddenly became a distant memory, just a memory. This is what my clumsy detective achieved: he resurrected you, and because of it, I am today less of a stranger in this world.

"What's more, now, when you must be asleep because of the difference in time zones, I feel as clearly as the early sun that touches the window before me that life has offered me the chance to stand before you again. Who knows when or where, but I feel in my body that we will meet again, and the mere thought brings tears to my eyes. But no, I won't cry, I won't waste my tears, I will save them to heal your wounds.

"Now I must keep going, I want to tell you how you were born and how you lived, who you were until you were stolen from me. That is, plain and simple, the purpose of all this: to let you know that your father's wife is not your mother. I must refute the things they told you that have led you to call your stepmother your mother

even though to achieve my goal I must bare truths that are
not to my liking."

L puts a small red cross on the Caracas map, at the
place where the children live. The neighborhood is on the
south side of town, on the southeast side to be exact, even
though the road she had to take to get to the hotel suggests otherwise.

It's late, dinnertime, but she isn't hungry. She has
taken off her pants and is wearing just her t-shirt. She
sniffs her armpits and takes her shirt off over her head. The
jacket and skirt from the other day, but nothing more, are
still in the wardrobe. She starts toward the bathroom, but
finally stretches out on the bed after making sure that the
door is locked. When she picks up the notebook from the
small table beside the bed and puts it on her naked belly,
she notices that her skin is moist. She removes the notebook from her belly and puts it on the sheets. She would
like to write, but doesn't have anything to say, except that
the children kissed their father and she found the address.
It doesn't seem like much. For an instant she entertains
the thought that she could ask for help at the address to
which she sent the letter earlier—please, I'm alone and
far from home, or something like that—but the thought
goes no further than that. It stops there, hanging in the
heavy, ever-simmering Caracas air. She has always been
talkative, or at least that's what she's been told since she
was little, and maybe they were right. At this moment
that's the most urgent need she feels, the need for some-
body to talk to.

She picks up the notebook and begins to read again.

"We were married the year Franco died, just then, one week later. Your father wanted to live with me, he wanted to form a new family, and your grandmother took this to be a reason for us to get married. The poor woman wouldn't have understood our reasons for not getting married. What did it matter to me to give in to the government in this as well? Marriage for me was similar to filling out the paperwork to get an identification card. Well, by now you know how convincing your father can be, all the more so when he's lying through his teeth.

"So, a week after Franco died we were married with hardly any ceremony. I was twenty-eight and your father was thirty. We lived in a neighborhood of San Sebastian, in the house that I was renting at the time. Your father was a mechanic and I was a teacher. And we had been involved in the same fight for a long time, the fight against the dictatorship and for the freedom of our people.

"Those were happy years, completely happy, and maybe I got drunk on that flood of happiness. I was in a hurry, wanting to live every day as if it were my last. Now it seems to me that rather than hurrying, I was fleeing, that I was afraid of normality. But that occurs to me only now, now that I long for ordinary life.

"So we got married and at the same time we decided that it was too early to have children, that those months were giving us the opportunity to change the direction of history and that was our first priority. Don't think it was easy; our reasons were substantial, crafted and debated, not just any old slap-dash reasons.

"But a year after we were married, I got pregnant. One morning, on my way to work, I felt ill. A couple weeks would pass before I would be able to determine the source of my illness, but that morning in the bathroom, as my body was trying to expel even more than it contained, I realized that I was pregnant. It was you, Miren, or the seed of the seed that would be you.

"Until the doctor confirmed my suspicions, I didn't tell your father anything. I thought he wouldn't appreciate the surprise and he would blame me and hold me responsible for what had happened; I thought he wouldn't take the news well. At that time your father planned everything, he tried to control the craziness around us by making plans, and even though those plans failed for the most part, he didn't give up, not at all. As soon as one scheme was frustrated, he'd come up with a new one without losing heart.

"I remember how and when I told him I was pregnant. We were waiting for a meeting to start, at the main entrance of the town hall of San Sebastian. The winter wind had driven us to seek shelter under the arches, and there, shivering with the cold, he said I didn't look so well. At once, I told him why, my right hand in my pocket, clutching the paper that said I was pregnant. As soon as he had heard what I said, your father hugged me. We'll look after it together, he said, placing his hands on my belly under my raincoat, and his mother would also help. If the old sayings are true, he said then, it'll be a girl, that's why you look so terrible, darling.

"Then they opened the doors and the meeting started. Soon we'll be a real family, he said that night on the way home. Days passed, weeks, my belly started to expand, but our life didn't change in any fundamental way. Work, meetings, sleep, work again, meetings, sleep, and once in a while, not often, dinner with friends.

"Except for those first few weeks, Miren, you didn't give me any trouble in my whole pregnancy. When it was still impossible to guess that I was pregnant if I didn't say so, the morning sickness stopped and from then on you peacefully took over my body: you governed my breasts, my waist, my belly, and even my face. Naturally, you grew naturally, I can't think of a better word. Like the beech trees in front of the window that need only time to grow.

"So in those months, we kept up the same pace as before, maybe with even more energy than ever. We were two, that was clear from the beginning, but each there for the other. Sometimes, in the middle of a meeting or at school, I felt a kick, always up high, but normally you moved when I was lying down, as if you didn't want to cause any trouble. You were there, Miren, snug and comfortable inside me, and sometimes I even forgot I was pregnant.

"That was the summer of marches for freedom and on the day of the last march, you were due in two weeks' time. I forget exactly what we were doing when the police burst upon us, but I see the people running like in a black-and-white movie, surrounded by the dirty fog of smoke canisters, people fleeing in all directions, and me running downhill, alone, down a hard and unfamiliar hill, holding my belly with my hands and arms, but not afraid, no, not a speck of fear. When the smoke started to disperse, I ran into your father and I've never forgotten that hug. You started kicking and I brought your father's hand to my belly. We were three.

"Girls, two; boys, one, said the doctor when you emerged from my belly, big and strong, more than seven and a half pounds, totally bald. You even cried elegantly from the very beginning. Blue eyes from the beginning and chestnut hair not long after."

L closes the notebook as if her curiosity were satisfied. I'm in your hands, Mother had told her, and that she
would have to decide for herself whether or not to read
the notebook.

Before falling asleep she thinks that maybe, because so
many years have passed since she lost her children, Mother
has lost her reason, that the love overflowing from the
notebook is too much, an obsession. But this idea doesn't
last for long. She immediately tells herself that she's not
a judge, but Mother's advocate. An honest person, she
remembers, and immediately hears the sweet voice of a
man asking what is this all about, taking a vacation alone,
who knows what you've gotten yourself into. She didn't
tell him where she was going or why, of course, but under
the obvious irony she feels calm, as if the man would take
care of her. She can almost imagine that she sends a message to him, I'm in Caracas and in danger, for example,
and, like Superman, the man comes to offer help.

The next day she doesn't wake easily, even though she
realizes where she is and what she's doing before she opens
her eyes. The trace of a nightmare she can't remember
doesn't disappear when she reviews the plan of the day.
So she dresses in the clothes she brought on the plane and
gets the car without eating breakfast, the city map folded
on the seat next to her.

It's half past ten by the time the place where the children live appears before her. She enters the building with
a black folder in her hands, no doorkeeper in sight. Without seeing anyone, she takes the elevator to the eighth
floor, having read the number on the mailbox. Eighth
floor, apartment B. As soon as she sees herself in the mirror, it occurs to her that she should change her appearance
a bit, and without hesitation, she takes a black ponytail

holder from her purse. By the eighth floor she has pulled back all her hair, gathered it at the nape of her neck.

As soon as she gets out of the elevator, she sees apartment B on the right and as soon as she takes two steps in that direction, she hears the children's dog barking. Apartment B is open and in the place where the wooden door should be, she sees a strong iron gate. The rat-like dog barks at her from the gate, and she thinks the house might be empty, but no, on the other side of the gate she sees the woman who was driving the old van the other day, carrying a small child in her arms.

A strand of the woman's hair is escaping, the cloth that held it coming loose down her back, and she is startled to see L before the door. L tells the woman she has come from the town hall to ask a few questions, and the woman answers that she should come back in the afternoon, her husband is at work and she won't be able to answer. Come back in the afternoon. The dog has gone quiet and the child wants to be put down, but the woman won't let go. Come back in the afternoon, she repeats, and L spreads an apparently believable smile across her face even though it's completely false. After this expression, she explains to the woman that the questions are simple, she's conducting a questionnaire to find out what the neighborhood needs. The woman hasn't gone away, but before answering the first question she closes her naturally small eyes until they are nothing but two black slits in her face. She has three children, the woman answers: the oldest is thirteen, the middle one ten, and the little one almost two, and yes, she was born in Caracas and so were her children. When L asks about her husband, the woman gets scared again, and returns to her earlier refrain: better to speak with her husband. Then she places her hand on the open door and, excusing herself, says she's going to close it.

L doesn't even have time to say thank you, and shouts that she'll come back in the afternoon. Then, without waiting for the elevator, she takes off down the stairs, infected by the woman's fear. Thank God the woman didn't ask for proof that she was with the city government. She calms down once she's in the car again, and on the way to the hotel thinks that maybe Mother is right, maybe they really did steal her children, and the doubt revealed by this thought surprises her. Surprises her and then shames her. And the shame lasts long hours, holding tight to her mind. It is still there after her lunch of rice at the Chinese restaurant across the street when she sets off for the school. She achieved more than a little, but she didn't prepare well, and too much was put at risk. Now the woman knows her and knows that she's not from there, knows that L has the same accent as her husband, even though she believed the lie about the town hall.

After parking the car behind the school, she climbs the stairs that seem pretentious from the top as well, and goes into the office that's right at the entrance. She tells the woman typing there that she's looking for a school for her fourteen-year-old daughter for the next semester and has come for information. Half a minute later, she's in a small office, listening to the information given to her by an elderly nun. Apparently there's no better school in all of Venezuela, and the nun has plenty of proof. Life is difficult these days, says the nun, and L doesn't contradict her. The sermon looks like it will be a long one and L cuts it off by asking what activities they offer outside of normal school hours. Dance, catechism, basketball, and gymnastics. All for a bunch of bolivars that, for the first

time since L has been in Caracas, seems very expensive.
The van may be old and run-down, but the children go
to a good school. Of course, it's a religious school, and L
knows that Mother wouldn't have chosen it.

L leaves after saying goodbye to the nun; it is half an
hour before the children will be out of school. She waits,
even though she has no particular plan to follow them.
When the time nears, the cars make a long line on the
left. By a quarter past five the line has dissolved, but L
hasn't seen the children. After deciding to wait until six
o'clock, she crosses the street, seeking shade. She takes
refuge under a tree with white flowers, and doesn't immediately feel any cooler, but she does notice an unfamiliar
sweet smell. The tree has lovely flowers, like camellias but
smaller, not as lavish. Besides, camellias don't smell.

It is five minutes to six when she sees the old van. The
woman is driving and, from where L stands, it looks as if
she has changed her hair style, just as L has. A short while
later, she sees the girl's face at the top of the stairs. The girl
sees the van and moves backwards, no doubt looking for
the boy. She appears again immediately, leading the boy
by the hand, pulling him forcefully until the boy gives in
and walks by her side. Then she puts her arm around his
shoulders. In her other hand she carries two sport bags,
swinging them.

After the van disappears, L enters the school again. In
the office they tell her that that day they have gymnastics,
boys and girls both.

A short while later, she is sitting on a sort of terrace
inside a shopping mall, drinking papaya juice. It's air-
conditioned and the hum of the people is pleasant. She is
tired of the solitude of the hotel and also a little afraid of
the notebook. She looks around at the shops within her

sight and thinks she could just as easily be in Madrid. The
La Vaguada mall comes to mind, but she immediately
censors the name and the meetings she had there. She has
known from the start that it's better to forget details completely, so that no one can read them in her mind.

She takes a stroll after she finishes her juice, but without going into the shops. The setting seems familiar, but
not the people. She feels like a stranger, and awkward
among so many women dressed well from head to toe.
She buys two postcards, for her mother and father. She
hasn't seen them for a long time and suddenly feels like
getting in touch. The notebook hasn't made her think of
the sons and daughters she doesn't yet have, but it is making her think of her parents.

It is Saturday morning and hasn't been light for long
when L arrives in front of the house where the children
live. She parks the Opel and then, slowly, as if she were in
no hurry at all, puts a tape in the cassette player and opens
the bag on the seat beside her. She takes all sorts of things
out of it, like a magician from a top hat: an unopened
packet of cigarettes, a notebook with a black cover, a copy
of the newspaper *Le Monde*, cookies, candies. No one is
on the street and, afraid of falling asleep, she picks up a
small book of crossword puzzles after putting the notebook on one side.

Nearby barking startles her and the clock shows that
she's napped for an hour. Before she knows it, the children's ugly dog is looking at her through the window she
fortunately did not roll down, and the father is only a
few inches away, calling the dog. He even says something,
looking into the car, but the barking doesn't stop and she
doesn't understand a word. Frozen in her seat, she sees the
man, the dog, and the girl going down the hill.

Caught unawares and heart still beating hard, she has to rein in the urge to reprimand herself. Time for that later, she thinks, and starts the car, but immediately turns the key the other way. The father and daughter left on foot, and in this city no one goes anywhere on foot. She was right: they soon return with the dog behind them, the father carrying a newspaper under his arm and the girl swinging a white plastic bag in her right hand. They are right in front of her, climbing the hill without rushing. They are talking, smiling. L thinks a person is missing from the image framed by the car window, maybe two. If she looked a little to the left, she would see Mother as she has never seen her except through the words in the notebook.

As the pair go into the building, L admits to herself that she doesn't like what she saw. Of course, it's better for the girl to have a good relationship with her father, and she thinks of her own father, who has not yet received the postcard she wrote, as he was when they lived together, face without wrinkles yet. If the extravagant sun here doesn't revive me, nothing will, she wrote to him the night before.

Time seems to creep by, but it has just turned twelve o'clock when she sees the black van heading down the hill. She didn't see it come out of the garage, but that's it, without a doubt. She starts the car and flings everything from her lap to the floor, roughly, carelessly. The Coke, which is warm by then, splashes her skirt before falling on the passenger seat. She doesn't worry about details, it's hard enough just to follow the van. Soon they're on the highway, of course.

Even without getting too close, L can see that the vehicle is full. The whole family, she thinks, and while she has the van in sight, she tries to clean up a little around her. She is not nervous, but she has yet to put a name to this buzz that she has felt only infrequently before now. I know it well, very well, Mother told her when she mentioned it to her, I call it the hunter instinct.

Even though she paid little attention to the route into the city from the airport when she arrived at Caracas, it seems to her now that she's going back out, and sure enough, soon she begins to see signs for the airport. The van, however, goes on another few kilometers. The hare leaves the highway without signaling and with the hound on its tail, with more and more misgivings because the roads taken by the van are getting narrower by the kilometer, as if the driver were always choosing the narrowest road at each intersection.

Macuto, says an old sign where the van turns into a parking lot at the side of the road. L goes on ahead, but not far. Without getting out of the car, she sees the father and the daughter entering a supermarket that's right there, and a short time later they come out laden with bags. The boy helps them stash their purchases. The wife doesn't move from her seat.

The van seems tired when it starts up again, but it doesn't matter because it stops immediately on the side of a road barely wide enough for two cars, right tires on the grass. L has to go on ahead and she hates to leave the Opel. Finally, she parks haphazardly and runs back, heart telling her that she's lost the trail.

Her heart was lying, and the van she followed for so many kilometers looks like a tame beast or a faithful dog when she spies it by the side of the road. Just in front of it, there is a small wooden door in the middle of an overgrown hedge. The family is here, no doubt about it, and L doesn't know what to do. She can't stop there to wait in the middle of nowhere. She looks around and sees that the sea is near, a few yards away, just down the hill. She heads that way without having decided anything, but stops short because she doesn't want to leave the place where the children are. She sits down on the ground and is aware that she no longer has the shelter of the car; it is as if she were unable to think without a roof over her head.

A familiar smell helps to calm her nerves. Looking up, she spots a tree like the one that gave her shade in front of the school and hanging from it, the flowers that she cannot name. She stays there, weary with hunger and humidity. It seems like years have passed since she left the hotel. If she stood up, she would see the sun glint on the abandoned van.

At five o'clock in the afternoon, she hears voices and laughter down the hill. She thinks it is Mother's voice before she remembers where she is and what she's doing. She hides behind the trunk of the flowery tree and from there sees about a dozen people jumping and playing as if their only salvation were the ocean. When she manages to calm the fear caused by her surprise, she looks down the hill. At the edge of the water, making a lot of noise, four children and a dog are playing. A little farther behind, some other adults and, at the point where the plants begin to do battle with the sand, the girl is sitting on the ground, arms around her legs. The girl is but a stone's throw from the others by L's calculation.

It doesn't look like enough. I can't just appear like an angel, speak, and disappear—I'm not the Virgin Mother; and, protected by words that haven't crossed her mind in a long time, she recalls a damp cave, as if she were the child Bernadette.

FOUR

"I took a short break and the dog that lives in the house where I am came over to me while I was in the kitchen making coffee. He came up with me and is now sitting by the side of the chair looking at me. No doubt he's hoping for something, but the lady of the house has forbidden me to give him anything to eat.

"Before starting again, I read what I've written so far without correcting anything, and I think before I continue my story, I'd better tell you a few things.

"There is basically one new concern: perhaps you've forgotten your Basque and you won't be able to read what I've written. Your father wouldn't do such a thing; this is what I pray in order to be able to go on.

"You were born and while you were with me, you were wholly immersed in Basque since your father and I are both native speakers. It was rarer in our time because there were few Basque speakers in San Sebastian when we were little. Anyway, for you the world existed in Basque—at home, at school, in the park by your grandmother's house, on television. Of course, I know that that doesn't guarantee that you still know Basque today, even if your father didn't erase your Basque like he did our relationship. I can learn to speak to you in Spanish, but not just now. If there's no other way, the person who gives you this notebook will translate.

"So Miren, my darling, you were born right in the middle of the campaign for amnesty and, before you were ten days old, you went to your first demonstration on my breast. Your father didn't come with us; he didn't think it was appropriate to take such a risk with a newborn. Your grandmother did come with us though, and perhaps since she had also gotten involved, I thought we were winning; they would have to give in to us soon, inevitably. Even now, that demonstration is among my favorite memories, at the very top of the list. I had your grandmother by the arm, you at my breast, going down the Avenue with everyone shouting with one voice. You woke up once, but it was before we all started running. Like one month earlier on Araba mountain, I ran with my arms tight around you, and you were asleep again by the time we took refuge in a bank with your grandmother.

"Don't worry, I do know the danger of recounting things by memory, I know the tricks memory can play. You think you explain any event as if it were far away, you just rewind the tape, there are no tricks. But you don't realize that, from one telling to the next, the images change just a little bit, a tiny bit each time, and if like me you replay the video endlessly for seven years, you have to recognize that you are no journalist. All of this doesn't contradict what I'm saying about the demonstration for amnesty: we were there, you were ten days old, and I thought and believed that we were arriving at the door to a new world.

"It was summer. Over Christmas I had been on vacation and it seemed to me that I had life itself on my side, that every obstacle had its good side. For example, my breasts never did have enough milk for your belly, and I had to give you first the breast, then the bottle. So sometimes your father gave you the bottle at night and I slept, as deeply as you did, I'm sure.

"When you started going to daycare, my life changed, but above all because I also started work. Your grandmother was against it and your father stayed carefully neutral. Your grandmother apparently felt sorry for you in strange hands. I didn't give in and your grandmother quickly got over her anger since you stayed with her when you were sick and other times as well. Sometimes you stayed there the whole weekend. You weren't your grandmother's first grandchild, nor the first granddaughter, but you were her pet, perhaps because she shared the responsibility for you.

"It's not hard for me to understand what your grandmother went through when your father disappeared with you, and I will always be grateful to her for giving me the key to finding you. The things she had to do to get the news to me weren't easy for a woman of her age, but she didn't shrink from the task. But that's another story, a branch that twists and turns as soon as it emerges from the trunk.

"You often stayed at your grandmother's house, but you often came with us, hanging onto us as we went from one place to another from the time you were born. I must say, your father was a leader in that and many other things. But I don't want to write much about your father, I'm not ready yet. In all these years, I've had every thought and feeling there is about your father. I thoroughly investigated the theory that you had all three died together, and many other possibilities. If they're alive, they'll come back to me, I thought, and your father was not included in that plural form. I know that these feelings that I am still unable to overcome can only do me harm from now on, but they exist and I don't want to deny them. I need time, I need to reconnect with you, not with him. So it is possible that my memory has censored your father from some of my recollections. If that is the case, blame it on my memory, not my will."

L doesn't know if reading the notebook is doing her any good, or even if it's necessary for her to read it. I came to do a favor for a friend, she thinks, not to decide who is right, she has to repeat to herself too often.

The family she saw in Macuto looks ordinary to her, a group of people like those she was so jealous of when she was little and that now inspire only indifference. This also carried a certain weight in her relationship with Mother, since for one thing she knew few women capable of living without family and ever since she was young, that is, ever since she perceived the problems between her parents, having and maintaining a family seemed a lot like slavery for women to her. Mother didn't suffer that captivity; she wasn't in anyone's clutches, or that's what L thought until Mother told her about Caracas. This is why the notebook scares her, because it is showing her a hidden side of someone she thought she knew well.

She's been poking around for a week and has yet to see any openings. Outdoors is no good because the girl never goes out alone. The school seems like the best chance, but she doesn't know how to play it there either. She turns the possibility of gymnastics over in her mind for a long time, but hasn't got the nerve to claim to be a gymnast, nor a coach either. To tell the truth, she's never loved sports, it's always seemed like an odd way to spend time, a way of wasting energy.

Perhaps it would be sufficient to give the girl a note, at the door of the school, at the top of the stairs, somewhere

where she's out of the sight of the driver of the van. She decides that, if all else fails, there will always be time to write the girl a letter and that first she has to eliminate a few other possibilities having to do with the school. *School*, she writes in felt-tip pen in the notebook with the black cover.

She notices then just how much more difficult everything is in a foreign country. Of course there are things that are easier than at home, but L doesn't think about that. How difficult everything is in a foreign country, she thinks, and after slinging her bag over her shoulder, goes out, thinking that if nothing else, seeing other people will clear her mind.

She gets out of the elevator and goes over to the reception desk to leave her key. She's about to step outside when she hears someone calling her from behind. *Señora, señora*, she hears, but she doesn't turn her head. The armed man at the exit is calling her *señora* and now she does get scared, as if the man who is talking to her were a statue come to life. They got me, she thinks, and turns around.

Her instinct has failed her this time—a bellboy is holding out her lost suitcase. Her originally fake smile turns into a real one. She takes the key and goes back up to her room with the bellboy behind her. She opens the suitcase on the bed and takes out first a blue dress, the color of the evening sky, then a red skirt and jacket. She puts them all on as if they were someone else's. She remembers that Mother always praised her taste in clothes and more than once gave her something that she had used, skirts and dresses, since even though they're fifteen years apart, they are almost the same size. Of course clothes are different on different bodies; everyone has their own style.

She goes out dressed in red from head to toe, like she used to go to local festivals, and the mirror in the elevator tells her she made the right choice. As has happened most times, the weight of the air takes her by surprise when she goes outside. The sky is half hazy, but the clouds are vertical rather than horizontal. If I were in the Basque Country, I would say a storm wasn't far off, she thinks, and that maybe she should take the car. The desire to walk wins out and she heads around the back of the hotel, looking for a park two blocks away.

That's where she is when she hears the first rumble of thunder and, looking up to the sky, she feels drops of rain. She looks for a tree and chooses one like the one in front of the school, with fragrant white flowers. The rain seems to turn to steam as soon as it hits the ground.

She remembers that once when she was little, she got caught in a thundershower going down Main Street with Ixabel holding her hand, and she refused to take cover under a roof or under the arches of the town hall. Her aunt had sent them to the sewing shop for thread, and even after so many years she can still feel her pleasure in being wet and the slap on the head from her aunt. That's why she leaves her shelter and goes out to feel the rain on her skin. She doesn't look around to see if anyone is looking; she has her head tipped back and her eyes closed.

She's soaked through when she goes into a bar across from the park, and before she looks around the place, she shakes her head like a dog, until her curls cover her face. It feels like night inside the place even though it's only dusk outside, and if she had been at home, she would never have gone into such a place alone. She goes to the bar and asks for a rum punch because that's what the sign says, that they make the best rum punch in Caracas there. The customers are few and the place is filled with the saddest music. Chavela Vargas, she realizes almost immediately.

"Chavela Vargas," says a man's soft voice on her right. The owner of the voice looks too young to be a fan, but a second look shows her he's not as young as she thought. They start talking and it seems to L that she is in a movie, in the hands of a director she must obey. The man is also a singer, but is not from Venezuela. He looks Mexican to L, not that she's an expert. Not everything is more difficult abroad she thinks when the man tells her he's Mexican.

"Spanish," she answers, not without feeling a bit of shame. She thinks she's blushing but there's no way to check. The man says he works for Televisa, and L understands that he must be talking about a Venezuelan channel. Without mincing words, she tells him that since she's been in Caracas she's seen something two or three times that amazes her, a slimming contest, and the man tells her that the women from there have an incredible problem with that and that there are worse things on television. She doesn't give a precise answer when the Mexican asks her what she's doing in Caracas: she's a tourist, and while she's there, she's doing a bit of business. This satisfies the man's curiosity and he immediately says she should change her clothes as soon as possible. For some reason L doesn't understand, most men want to protect her, they act fatherly toward her. They make a date for the next day, for dinner. She doesn't know how it happened, but it did.

It has stopped raining by the time she leaves and the clothes plastered to her body give her a long shiver. On her way back to the hotel, it occurs to her that the Mexican may be just what she was looking for. She agreed to the date for the next day without thinking about this, and feels that she's on the right track.

As soon as she gets back to the room and without taking off her clothes, which are still damp, she picks up the black notebook and writes the word *school* in it, and below it *gymnastics*; then she writes the word *report*, with a circle around it. When she starts sneezing, she remembers that the man had said she should change clothes, and she does. She gets into the tub and when she's under the shower it occurs to her that there's a better pretext than the gymnastics. She'll do a report on children with Spanish ancestry, she thinks, and the idea seems better and better.

Thinking that she's found the opening she was looking for, she goes to bed, with the Mexican on her mind. She doesn't know which would seem worse to Mother, the Spanish ancestry angle or the ease with which she took up with the man. Nevertheless, she feels proud as she goes to sleep.

By the time she wakes up, what seemed so possible last night has now fallen flat. She doesn't really care much what Mother will think later, but her father's opinion does matter. Before getting out of bed, she realizes she'll have to find another pretext—the Spanish ancestry idea won't do the trick. The woman with slits for eyes told her she had three children and, in the words of the first report to Mother, the school also thinks their stepmother is their mother. So their father will never go along with the ancestry report.

She paces the room from one side to the other as if walking will help her think. She picks up the black notebook and sits on the unmade bed, felt-tip pen in her right hand. On a new page she writes *school* again, and below it, after leaving a good-sized space, *report*. The candidates for the third word come to her slowly. *Gymnastics* again is the first, but that's a dead end.

While she has breakfast in the coffee shop downstairs, she keeps turning it over in her mind, staring into the distance. Finally, when she least expects it, in the elevator, the children's dog comes to mind. Dogs. When she first starts thinking about it, it seems too simple, but on second thought that's the best thing about the idea: its simplicity. Nothing else occurs to her in the half-hour she spends with the notebook after breakfast.

She sticks with the dog idea, turning it over in her mind in the absence of anything else. Perhaps, if the Mexican is willing to help her, she'll find a better pretext. There must be one; she's sure of that.

"You were almost a year old during that vacation, in 1978, on June 24 when you started walking, suddenly, almost without practice, on the feast of Saint John, as if you had been waiting for my holidays to start. And from the very first day, you walked with great assurance, almost without falling. You did everything like that, with great deliberation, in the words of a friend I saw a lot of at the time.

"As soon as you learned to walk, you developed a great desire to go out, and as soon as you had eaten breakfast or lunch, you stood up and led me to the door, like dogs do, without words. And I obeyed you most of the time. We often took the bus and went to the beach in Gros, if it wasn't raining.

"That summer you started walking, I met the organization, my future. The person who gives you this notebook will give you the details that I must keep quiet. The thing is, the fight for amnesty, from demonstration to demonstration, from meeting to meeting, led me to other tasks, other meetings and other commitments.

"I didn't make any decisions from a position of knowledge, I made no calculations. It just happened, and as I write I realize that at that time, and also in the years that followed, it seemed to me that everything just happened naturally. I was on vacation, I had a daughter who did everything naturally, a husband who was also a friend and, thanks to your grandmother, I had plenty of time and freedom.

"That August your father and I went on vacation, leaving you with your grandmother. We drove all the way to Paris, even though your father would rather have taken the train. We went for a week, and I bet it was harder for him than for me not to see you, Miren, for so many days. We thought Paris was beautiful, witness to a better world, and the days flew by. Even so, we were happy to go home, and we didn't stop on the way; we were anxious to get back to you. We were happy, proud because even though we were parents, we were also a couple. Or that's what we said to each other—I remember it clearly—as we drove through the pine groves of Les Landes. I think at that time your father even admired me. He didn't have many details of my new relationships and responsibilities, but he supported them, totally, and always said he couldn't do it himself, he wasn't brave enough. I, however, had no fear, nor, therefore, the energy to jump over that black hole.

"You will have realized by now that every time I have to mention your father, that's how I write it, *your father*, never his name. I know that that's a problem of mine, that this hatred that he caused in me by taking you away has hurt me these many years. I don't know what sort of journey you made from my arms to that school in Caracas, but at least I have been able to verify that you are with your father, and that's no weak pretext to make me rethink this thing with your father. Your photo has upset me; you, Beñat, seeing how much you look like your father gave me a quite a shock. Now I know that feelings of hatred harm not your father but me.

"So that summer, you were no problem, Miren, but rather the person who spurred on our joy. Even the need to return soon to work didn't dampen our mood. What a hardworking family, your grandmother used to say with a smile, but with a little sadness in her eyes.

"When autumn came, life returned to normal or, at least, normal for the school year. As you see, my memories are well classified, chronological; I know what I was doing when you, Miren, started talking, or when you, Beñat, stood for the first time. Undoubtedly, these seven years of drought and my own way of life have led me to this point, for I have spent too many years seeking love to be always looking back. But your early years are there in my mind, well classified and archived, if you ever want to ask.

"I remember at the beginning of the school year a co-worker gave me a book about children's language. You, Miren, met all the norms, you put words together or made sentences just when the book said you would. *Man work*, you said at just barely two years old, your first sentence, when some workers were crossing the sidewalk in front of our house. The book's foreword said that we learned what we know about children's language because of the work done once linguists became parents, and even though I wasn't a linguist, I enjoyed watching your progress. I know exactly where the notes that I took on the topic were at that time, when I had to leave home: in an old cabinet we had in the living room next to the balcony. I don't want to think where they must be now, where your father left or threw those papers that were so important to me."

L falls asleep without realizing it, without having eaten lunch. Hunger wakes her, and there is the red notebook, still open, but she doesn't keep reading. Since she fell asleep, she doesn't have time to go see the children, and even though she doesn't know what use it would be to hang around in front of the school, it feels like she made a mistake. Too many mistakes, she thinks, when her brain produces a long list: not wearing a disguise to talk to the stepmother, the dog practically jumping into her car . . .

She doesn't want to go down that road, so she starts thinking about the evening, deciding what to wear. She felt rich when they returned her suitcase to her yesterday, but time moves at a different pace since she's been in Caracas. Now it seems to her that the clothes she brought are not appropriate for what she has to do. She would like to wear a low-cut dress or at least a jazzy shirt. She even thinks of going to the shop next to the Chinese restaurant, but immediately squelches the temptation.

Finally, she puts on a tight black dress and ties a flowery silk cloth around her waist, hugging her right hip, seeking to soften the bones that recently seem too much to her. She even thinks she might not go, so she leaves the room quickly. The glances she receives on her way to the park do nothing to calm her down and, when she reaches the tree that sheltered her the night before, she unties the cloth and drapes it over her shoulder. Thank God I didn't buy anything new, she thinks, and sits down on a bench. She has twenty minutes to do the preparation that really matters.

The setting sun will use the time to complete its task. Of course, she can't tell the Mexican the truth, but she has begun to learn that it's not easy to choose the right size of lie. The night before, when she hadn't decided about the report, she told him she was a tourist, but also a lawyer and that she was doing some research for a client. She feels like backing out at the last minute but she thinks she can't do it all alone. What a puritan I am when it gets right down to it, she thinks, and thus stands up and ties the cloth around her waist again.

And now a rum punch, easy conversation, meaningful glances and a taxi to a restaurant. The Mexican says there's a huge difference between Mexican and Venezuelan food, but one can't leave a place in good conscience without tasting its food. He laughs to hear that L has had lunch most often in a Chinese restaurant.

The restaurant the man has chosen is not very big, but the owner hasn't put too many tables in it. They talk about food for a long time. The man is clearly educated, able to say or ask something appropriate about anything. He asks a lot of questions when she says she's Basque, for example, but his curiosity is relatively well-informed.

While they are eating, the Mexican says that many things can be learned without asking a thing; for example, he would guess that she's about thirty years old and unattached. To tell the truth, until she heard this last sentence, L thought she was part of a couple. She immediately understands, however, that the Mexican is right, and the wound doesn't hurt at first. Bingo, L answers.

After saying she has no room for dessert, L chooses ice cream. She confesses to herself that, contrary to what she had thought, the evening wasn't difficult at all. She didn't mention the report because she feels there's no hurry. The man decides that they will have their dessert and coffee at a table outside, and they go out to the back patio, with the man leading the way. Before L sees them, she smells the flowers she knows so well by now, but the man doesn't know what they're called. The waiter does, even though he doesn't immediately understand the question. "Frangipani," he says, or something like that.

As soon as they sit down again, L tells the man that she needs his help. And yes, men always like to be helpful to women. She tells him that she needs photos for a report she's doing, good photos, professional ones; her client is looking for some children and she found them there, in Caracas. The man asks if she's a detective, and gets a real laugh for an answer. L explains that she's not doing anything illegal, they'll take the pictures at a nuns' school, not in the middle of the street or secretly.

How much will it cost, more or less, to hire a camera for a couple hours, a camera, a photographer, and a journalist, so that they will believe it's for a report for a local channel; that's what L wants to know, and the man says he doesn't know, but he can find out. Then they talk about using the report as a pretext. The man doesn't like the dog plan, at least not if she wants to go through the school. He tells her that children never take dogs to school, such a report would have to be done in a park or at a club. L didn't expect that answer, but she agrees that the man is right. On the other hand, when she mentions the gymnastics, the man immediately says yes, that sounds like a good idea.

Soon they have things wrapped up. The man promises he will tell her the next day how much she'll have to pay and that he'll ask in the editorial office for more information to round out the gymnastics angle. He doesn't speak at all brusquely, but L has the impression that he's one of those people who is used to making decisions at work. She suddenly understands that Televisa is not a local channel, but a Mexican one.

To finish the evening well, the man suggests that they go to hear a little music, and L wavers before answering. For one thing, she thinks, apart from work, it wouldn't do any harm to strengthen her relationship with the man, and for another, she has never made such a bold move before. Strengthen the relationship, she thinks, word by word, and sees herself making her bold move like never before. Like a man, she thinks proudly. She has always disdained safe paths but feared borders. It is difficult to cross borders, Mother said to her long ago, but the return trip is even more difficult. I won't know how to do it, she is afraid before answering about the music, I don't know how to act with Mexicans. She also thinks that she should dare to do it, for once in her life she should behave like a man.

L is still untangling this knotty problem when the man speaks again. He tells her that before she answers, she should know that she's speaking with a gentleman, a *caballero*, he wants to make that clear from the start. L is familiar with the word, even though she's never used it. The man says he's a *caballero*, but perhaps she doesn't understand the meaning of the word. The Mexican doesn't stop there, he tells her that he's married, he's the father of two beautiful children and he has no intention of abandoning his respect for his family. When he became a father, he promised himself he would never do anything he couldn't explain to his children, and he's never broken that promise.

By now, L doesn't know what to think or what to say. It feels like the man read her mind and her cheeks burn. Fortunately, the Mexican goes on, which allows her to regain a bit of calm.

He tells her he's not ashamed of what he said, for him it's a serious issue, he truly believes in that type of loyalty and it's hard for him, often incredibly hard, for physical reasons, if for no other reason.

Before she knows it, the man is talking about his son and daughter, and she certainly didn't expect that at all. He has pictures and everything in his wallet and he lays them out there, on the table under the frangipani, among the recently emptied dishes, one by one, as if they were the purest crystal. She should feel rejected, but she's too astonished.

The man pays for dinner and promises to show her what good eating is the next day. L, with what pluck remains to her, answers that the Basques know a little something about good eating, she will look for a Basque restaurant for another time. She says no to the music; knowing that there will be a next time has made her brave.

Apparently, thinks L in the taxi on the way back to the hotel, mine were the only parents in the world who didn't love their daughter. And she immediately decides that perhaps it wasn't lack of love, but lack of the kind of love she wanted.

"That school year had no winter, the only season that went by like lightning took us to May, and that May, while your father was away, I also had to leave several nights to sleep at your grandmother's house. That was my first hint of what would happen to me, and after talking to your father on the telephone, I made my decision. At school, I said I was sick and we spent sweet days safe at your grandmother's house, almost without going out, with the geraniums on the balcony already in flower. We slept in the same room, each one in her own bed, at first holding hands, dangling them over the whitish carpet between us.

"The difficult times didn't last long and soon, as soon as your father returned, the three of us were home, seeking normality. Your father told me that the most difficult aspect of all our issues was my lack of fear, that hominids would never have become humans if they had had no fear. I have not forgotten those discussions, because we had

long arguments about risk, and the upshot was that I had
to promise him that I would not take on too much that
summer. Not too much, I promised, and I tried to keep
that promise with reasonable success.

"That summer you said your *man work* sentence, and
with that achievement your father started talking about a
second child, gently but persistently, something like the
way women do. He had always told me he wanted at least
two children, at least, and that it was useless to leave it
up to me. I understood what he meant, and I pretended
to agree. To tell the truth, you were so easy, Miren, I had
no doubt that the same thing would happen with the
second one.

"It was early in the eighth year of the decade when
I found out I was pregnant. Or to be more precise, your
father figured it out before I did, and that was when I
found out that he had been tracking my periods since the
summer. Your father welcomed you, Beñat, by saying
it was about time. He told me I was beautiful, and how
wonderful, that's exactly what he wanted, a boy. We'll
always have a girl one time, then a boy the next, he said,
happy as could be.

"Despite what I had hoped, my pregnancy with you,
Beñat, was difficult, almost from the beginning. At the
end of a lockout at the Good Shepherd church I was overcome by great exhaustion. I lay down on one of the church
pews with your father at my side, but in the middle of an
argument. You started to kick, Beñat, for the first time,
and even before happiness could overtake me, my womb
clenched, without pain but for a long time. With my
hands on my belly, I tried to calm you. I want out, I want
out, you seemed to be saying, and then, then I got scared.
There were still about four months to go, and quietly but

clearly, I explained to you that coming out now was the worst option for both of us.

"You calmed down at last, my womb returned to its former state, but over the next few days the same thing happened again. Until the doctor put me on bedrest. From bed to toilet and toilet to bed, he said; and that's what I did: I took a taxi, went home and went to bed. And there I stayed, lying on my back, hands on my belly and eyes welling with tears. You, Miren, were with your grandmother, and your father was at work. I stayed there for a long time, without calling anyone. I didn't think I would be able to speak without crying, and at that time I was ashamed of tears, mine or anyone else's. That's exactly what happened when I called your grandmother, she couldn't understand a thing through my tears. Anyway, I called and a few minutes later, there was your grandmother with you, Miren, by the hand.

"For three months, that bed was our nest, my workplace, and our play area. I had three caretakers, and I needed all three through the first days and weeks. I had said from the beginning that I didn't need another child just then, but I was pregnant and I didn't want to lose the baby who was coming to us. The next days passed in tears. I shed tears even while dreaming, in floods, and the tears flowed so fast that I couldn't believe the sheets were dry when I woke up. When I was awake I can honestly say I didn't forget my pregnancy for one second, that I felt every moment that the one inside me needed my body and blood to stay alive. Not to mention when I was dreaming.

"Then, little by little, things settled down, and before that July was over, I had even come to enjoy having to stay in bed. Around me, I had the telephone, the radio, the television, a notebook like the one I'm filling today, a load of books, your grandmother and you, Miren. Your father too, of course, but he left home early in the morning and returned late. From time to time, you went out with your grandmother, Miren, and went to the beach too, once I started to lose my fear of being alone.

"You have to give in to time, your grandmother used to say, because it's hopeless and harmful to fight it. And I tried, even though I didn't know exactly how to. I read, I listened to the radio. Sometimes, when I liked the music they were playing, I put the little radio on my belly and it seemed to me that you liked it, Beñat, that it calmed you better than anything else.

"I spent hours listening to my body, examining it as if it were someone else's. And actually, it was someone else's, yours, that is, Beñat. I also wrote down the thoughts that went through my mind in my notebook and, even though I blush now to use the word, poems, to the coming baby. When your father ran away with you, I lost that notebook together with a number of books and papers that I had accumulated over the years.

Ever since I was little, I had collected everything: papers, photos, concert tickets, postcards, letters, as if in order to move forward I had to leave a trail of bread crumbs behind me. Then when I lost everything, I was no longer in a situation that allowed me to collect things. I lack nothing essential, but this room is not mine, nor is the radio I listen to or the dog that seeks my company when I go to the kitchen. All of my things can fit into a medium-sized suitcase, and they do, often.

"Then, however, I had no need of a suitcase, I was rich and felt it; rich, cared for, loved, and therefore able to offer love to others. I wrote sentences like that too in that notebook, and when you asked me what I was writing, Miren, I told you I was writing stories, but they weren't finished yet, I had more work to do."

L doesn't want to go on or isn't able to; most of the time it's the same old things anyway. After turning off the light, the Mexican comes to mind, of course, how it frightened her not to have made any progress, as if she had sensed what was coming, the cheap lyrics he sang about his kids, and how finally she too was infected with the man's love for his children. He didn't give you the chance to make your move, she thinks, but at least it occurred to you and you made the decision. For the first time in your life, you didn't just stand there waiting. It occurs to her that it's reason enough to remember the Mexican, there are less worthy people who don't leave her memory. Just then she realizes that the man who would come to her aid like Superman was also there in her memory, in the past, sent there by the Mexican. And she doesn't feel alone, but free.

Then the last words she read in the notebook come to her mind, the part about having more work to do. And she falls asleep halfway through her list of plans for the next day.

FIVE

When she wakes up she feels no heaviness in her gut and no regret in her mind. She gets up and, before beginning anything, fixes a black coffee and dips some cookies into it. She has to add the cost of the report to the rental fee for the Opel, and she'd rather save as much as possible. Besides, she thinks she's gotten a bit thinner since she's been in Caracas and she wants to keep it up. Then she takes the shower she needed the night before and sits at the table with the black notebook before her.

Gymnastics, she writes again, and remembers the boy. She realizes that from the beginning, the girl has been her goal, maybe because that seemed easier to her. While she ponders, she makes little drawings around the word *gymnastics*, little stars and a moon. *Coach*, she writes next, and it occurs to her that in order to be able to round out what the Mexican will do, it wouldn't hurt to talk with the coach in advance. She doesn't know exactly what she'll gain, but she doesn't want to wait in the hotel all day.

She changes clothes two or three times before the mirror in the room to eliminate the impression that she was looking for a school for her fourteen-year-old daughter. She may have to talk to the Mother Superior this time too, and she doesn't want to repeat what happened with the stepmother. She can't change her accent as easily, and she knows that's what gives her away the most. It occurs to her to steal the Mexican's inflection because the Caracas accent can't be faked. She makes a couple of attempts in a low voice, until she feels a little more sure of herself. She chooses the red dress finally and gathers her hair in a bun, put up and pulled back, with her forehead and the nape of her neck showing, wide eyebrows that she always keeps covered now in the foreground.

She gets the car and goes to the usual shopping mall. There, in the same shop where she bought the postcards for her parents, she makes business cards. *LAURA GARATE*, she types into the computer in capital letters, and below it, *Editor-in-Chief of Channel 47* and the hotel phone number. When the machine spits out the printed cards, they look believable, even though she hasn't written an address.

The nun in the office tells her that she has to talk to the Mother Superior and she feels proud somehow that she adopted her idea of disguising herself. The Mother Superior's office is dark, with the blinds that were open last time almost completely lowered. The woman has L's card in her hands and L says right away that she's working on a report on the influence of gymnastics on the young and that, according to the information she's gathered, this school's coach is one of the best. The Mother Superior's face softens a little when she hears this praise and, without further ado, she says that the coach will be there that afternoon at five o'clock, and that L would do better to talk with her.

As she goes back out to the street, it occurs to her that the Mother Superior has kept her card, but this doesn't worry her. She'll do the report, she'll meet the girl and tell her about the red notebook. For the first time since she accepted the task in hand, her fear is less than her hap-

piness. She decides to stay out until she meets with the
coach, and goes right back to the CCCT shopping mall.
Thinking that what she has achieved deserves a prize, she
sits on the terrace and orders a papaya juice.

Before she has emptied the glass, it occurs to her that
it's one thing to be careful with money and another to be
miserly. It's a simple argument, but it helps. She wants to
buy a top, a tight t-shirt like the ones most young women
in Caracas are wearing, and especially high-heeled shoes;
she wants to see the world from higher up. She goes into
a shop called Europa in the CCCT to look and buys not
only pointy high-heeled sandals, but also two small t-shirts
and tight black pants. She would like to wear them, to see
as soon as possible the results of her transformation, but
she doesn't think it's appropriate clothing for the school.
The shoes, okay, so she wears them out of the shop and
moves forward step by step as if she were on a catwalk, one
foot in front of the other, backside jiggling delicately.

From then on, she doesn't pay attention to the insane
Caracas traffic, or maybe she drives more clumsily because
of the heels. Either way, the children have started coming
out of the school by the time she parks and arrives at the
door. She runs the last few yards before seeing the girl
alone at the top of the stairs. Not alone, talking to another
girl, but without the boy. As L goes up, she sees that the
girl is going down, talking non-stop with her friend and
not looking back, not even to the place where the van usu-
ally is. They pass each other in the middle of the staircase
and, once the girl is behind her, L turns around. From
there she sees the two friends heading off to the right.

L hasn't caught her breath yet, but she decides to go
after the two girls, even though she keeps in mind that the
Opel is poorly parked. When the girls disappear around a

corner to the right, L runs, or tries to, on the sharp heels she has yet to master. When she reaches the corner, she sees the two of them in line at a bus stop. L joins the queue, half hidden beside a young man who arrived after the girls.

When the bus comes, the dissimulation is impossible to keep up since you need exact change for the bus ticket, as the driver explains in a yell. L can't find the coins easily and as soon as she pays, she meets the girl's eyes. She sits down red-faced with her heart in her throat. Three stops further on the two friends get off and there, before the bus even moves on, they separate. The girl stays at the bus stop, apparently waiting for another bus, alone. L doesn't move. It seems to her that she is not ready to speak to the girl, that the whole thing will go bottoms up if she rushes it. She overcomes her distress when the bus sets off again, as if she had left the girl in the middle of the desert.

I haven't lost her, she has to repeat twice to herself. She takes down the hair she had gathered in a bun without thinking what she's doing. By the time her bangs are back to their usual place, her eyes are about to tear up. Thinking that her hair doesn't offer her enough of a hiding place, she puts on dark glasses and sheds a few tears behind them, warm and heavy.

L gets off at the next stop and first thinks of going by foot to meet the coach, but she hails a taxi because her shoes are shredding her feet. It's five minutes to six when she reaches the door of the school and, rushing and hurrying, she pulls her hair back as it was before. She goes to the office in this guise and from there to the gymnasium. She isn't limping, but by now she has cursed the new shoes more than once.

The coach listens gladly but without surprise to the bouquet of compliments L tosses her in a rush, as if long accustomed to receiving praise. Of course she is willing to have her work on television. She has just one condition—the parents' permission—and L promises that she will leave letters in the office the very next day for the parents of the girls that do gymnastics. When she asks who the best students are, the coach mentions five or six names without hesitating; and among them, the girl's. L writes down the names in the black notebook and takes her leave.

The coach has taken the bait, that's what matters to L, that she's gotten herself precisely on the right track to her goal. It seems to her that, despite the scars, it's worth it to see the world from higher up. She has a whole hour to get ready for dinner and even though her heels are burning, she knows she will wear the high-heeled shoes.

At the reception desk, together with her key, they give her an envelope, addressed to her: there, in blue pen, she reads her name, no last name. She doesn't have the patience to wait for the safety of her room, and she reads the page in the envelope in the elevator. It's from the Mexican, written to move the evening's date back an hour. The man doesn't say how he found her, and L thinks she'll ask him that first.

"By then you loved stories, Miren, like all children, but stories weren't the kind of narration you loved best. Often, in the evening, after dinner, freshly bathed and smelling of flowers, you would come to my side on the bed and your grandmother would tell us stories about the old days. Those were the exact words we used: stories about the old days. Your grandmother told with superb elegance how, when she was little, there were almost no cars on the streets nor televisions in the houses, and I don't know what was harder for you to believe, that your grandmother was also a child once or that the world wasn't always the way you knew it to be. Or she would tell war stories, how your grandfather was in jail for so many years or how they put your grandmother into prison when the bad guys won the war.

"You fell asleep without us realizing it most times, but every once in a while you said you wouldn't sleep unless your grandmother and I, together, told you the story of the little goldfish. And so your grandmother would start off telling the story of the little goldfish who had no friends. In turns, with your grandmother saying several sentences and me the next few, we would tell you that the little goldfish found a friend, someone that would be his friend forever. And then you would give in and close your eyes, smiling as if the little goldfish were tickling you. I told you both that very story that day in the pine grove, but after so many years, the little goldfish has surely died of sadness because you, who should have been his friends forever, have forgotten him.

"So you would fall asleep at my side and your grand-mother would retire to the kitchen, stiffly, to make our dinner. I stayed there, watching over your sleep, and Beñat too would calm down until your father arrived. Then your father would carry you to bed and we would eat together, in the room of course, telling each other what had happened that day. We had long conversations those evenings, without arguments or at least without getting angry. About politics too, often, about the worrying ways of the world, about our daughter or the baby that was soon to come. Once we talked about God, about baptism to be specific. You weren't baptized, Miren, and when you were born, we hardly discussed the issue. Your father said your grandmother would prefer that we baptize you, but your grandmother herself didn't say anything to me, and it seemed to me that there was no need to give in on this issue, that getting married was enough. You, Beñat, were about to be born when your father brought up the subject again, saying that your grandmother would be glad if you children were baptized, that perhaps she had already done it secretly with Miren. I said I couldn't believe that, that your grandmother deserved more trust, and that she would understand why we didn't baptize you. That's where it stayed, and your father didn't mention the issue again.

"Then too I used to say I couldn't imagine my parents talking so long about me, nor the grandmother who lived so near for so many years. We even started talking about you before you were born. And after you were born, any event, a question of yours, little Miren, or you, Beñat, how you fell asleep sucking your thumb, and we started talking, trying to guess what you would be like, what we had to do so that you would grow up to be good and honorable people. We can't protect them from everything, I often said to your father, and he said that he knew that, but that many things were in our hands, and that that commitment was unbreakable.

"In the meantime, Beñat, during that wearisome pregnancy I did everything I could, and so did you, of course, so that you would wait until later to come. I remember that I felt your movements the most in the afternoon, often when Miren was in the bath. Your desire to hurry was never satisfied. Take it easy, my love, I would pray with my hands immediately on my belly, and then I would tell you to wait, there were still six weeks to go, or four. I don't know why, by the end, it was always when I was alone that I felt your haste, Beñat, as if when I was with anyone else you didn't want to let it be known that you were in charge of my body.

"When you started moving, I turned on the radio, which was smaller than a pack of cigarettes. I always looked for a station that played classical music, and I would put the radio on my belly to try to calm your nervousness. Sometimes, the few times when I recognized the tune, I hummed because I thought that way the music would reach you two ways, from the inside and from the outside. And the system never failed, you always calmed down and I think often you fell asleep inside me, in the arms of the music.

"So we endured, sometimes in competition, other times the two of us working together, and unlike the first pregnancy, I felt every second I was awake that there was someone else inside me, that I was not the owner of my own body. You, Beñat, you were the owner and that feeling gave me no pain, nor did it lessen the love I had for your father and Miren.

"You were born ten days early finally, but healthy. It was in the afternoon and you, Miren, were at school. Your grandmother had gone to tidy her house a bit before picking you up, and your father was at work. I got up to go to the bathroom and as soon as I stood up I noticed I was getting wet. I'm leaking piss, I thought foolishly, but no, that wasn't it. We had already rehearsed many times what I should do if something like that happened when I was alone. I called your father and lay down on the floor, on some towels. Your father arrived immediately, bringing with him the calm sureness that I had seen in him since the beginning, and before I knew it, I was in the hospital. Two hours later it was all over and you, Beñat, were alive on top of me, not inside me. It's a tie, said your father, two men and two women. I should have written *tie* in the Basque that's being standardized so quickly, but your father used the Spanish word and then he said that now we were a real family.

"A few days later, when we went home, all three happy, all four happy, your father, not entirely joking, said that the only thing we needed now was a puppy. I myself needed nothing more; it seemed to me that the people who said that life was hard were exaggerating.

"In a few days, we went out for a walk. Autumn had come suddenly while I was in the hospital, with downpours and thunder. But it turned nice again immediately and I wanted to get out of the house. I hadn't felt such a thing the whole time I was in bed, not even close. Quite the opposite, I used to say that the media and the telephone were all I needed to stay in touch with the world. That autumn, however, I felt the walls closing in on me. Early in the morning, your father left with you, Miren, and as soon as you went to school, I got dressed, I dressed you, Beñat, and we went out for any reason or no reason, to visit your grandmother or something. I walked along the seafront, looking for familiar faces, wanting to show off my son to the world."

L thinks again that, since she came to Caracas, or actually since she accepted the job, the girl has always been on her mind; she has circled around her, without giving much attention to the boy, maybe because he was only three when they were stolen or because the girl is thirteen now. L hasn't been around children for a long time.

She is the daughter of divorced parents and has always thought she wouldn't have children. Small children seem fragile to her, brought into this world of too much suffering against their will. Anyway, it seems to her an error not to have cared more about the boy. Tomorrow, the boy, she decides.

The clock says it's time to get ready, and she goes to the shower, putting off the temptation to satisfy her curiosity about the boy in the notebook. While she's in the shower, Mother's face comes to her mind, as she looked when she asked L to spend her vacation taking care of Caracas.

You're never younger than today, she thinks, as she stands before the mirror in her new pants, red t-shirt and new shoes. Her wet hair falls in soft curls around her face and finally she gathers it up at the back of her neck, as she did when she went to the school. She wears the scarf she wore around her waist the night before over her shoulder, untied. Like a gypsy, her father would say if he saw her, and that gives her the bit of courage she needs to go out. An unknown instinct prompts her to scrutinize the faces of the people in the lobby and her favorite is the wet glance of the man at the reception desk. I'm going to work too, after all, she thinks.

On the street, she notices that the sun has lost most of its light, but not its ability to make the environment sultry. Her high heels make little holes in the asphalt and that doesn't make it any easier to walk.

When she enters the bar, she sees that the man is waiting for her, even though it's a few minutes before the time they set. Yes, the Mexican answers, he did his task, he's got the estimates in his pocket, and he points to his chest, the pocket just above his heart. She sees something in his gaze that wasn't there the night before and the desire for revenge makes her think that she should ask after his children right away. She doesn't do it, however, and starts off with small talk, the heat, the weather, the beggars on the street.

Unfortunately, the chosen restaurant is nearby and they go on foot, down a street full of people. These damned shoes are killing my feet, she thinks, and tries to walk gracefully for a couple yards. Then, when the man tells her that in order to reach the restaurant they must cross the small park in front of them, she takes her shoes off and goes barefoot on the soft lawn of the park. "I can't wear them any longer," she explains to the man, who is roaring with laughter. That's how they enter the courtyard of mariachi music, L carrying her shoes in her hand.

As soon as they choose a table and order, the man takes two folded white papers out of his shirt pocket, before L asks. She has two possibilities he explains, one simple and cheap and the other more complex and more expensive. Without asking what the difference is, L chooses the first. When he tells her how many dollars she will have to pay, she takes out the black notebook and does the math. She hasn't got enough dollars, even though she has used only bolivars from the beginning. Even using all the dollars she brought as emergency funds, she still doesn't have enough. The Mexican says they can easily remedy that, and L thinks she'll have to start wheeling and dealing, but no, the man says she can pay part of it in bolivars. She'll be left almost without a penny, but she can pay for a camera and a man to use it. The Mexican says he'll go too, to make the team look bigger to the school.

L would prefer to go to the hotel without further ado, but she stays, though her scant experience tells her that the *caballero* could renege on his agreement. And after finishing their business, the man does indeed try to gain a bit of intimacy. That happens with dessert, and the situation seems silly to L. She asks how he knew what hotel she was in, and the man confesses that the night before, secretly, he followed her. He regretted it later, both following her and going behind his family's back.

Sweetly, with a smile, leaning forward, L tells him she has to go because she's waiting for a call. Before standing up, she puts her shoes back on, even though she can feel that her heels are nearly bleeding. The man stays there when the waiter tells her that her taxi is waiting. She knows that calling for a taxi took the shine off the evening, but she can't go far on foot. Before she leaves, she tells the man twice that she will call him in the afternoon at the latest, as soon as she talks to the school. Inside the taxi, she takes her sandals off and doesn't question the worth of the whole evening since she arranged for the report. However, her final retaliation has left a bad taste in her mouth. She reminds herself that she's far from home and tries to think about something else because she doesn't like looking back, examining what has been done.

"It is precisely eleven o'clock," says the television from the room, and L is sitting in the tub soaking her feet. She is concentrating on her task and wants to read the notebook, she wants to get to know the boy, and besides, the part about the pregnancy is over. She confesses to herself that she was almost embarrassed to read that part; it seemed too physical, too intimate. For the same reason, she likes the idea about the boy; she can use it as an excuse. L gets up a short while later and, hardly drying her feet, steps onto the carpet in the room. Who would think to put in

wall-to-wall carpet in Caracas, thinks L as she takes off her
street clothes and puts on a camisole.

"I had plenty of free time since I didn't have to go
back to work until after the feast of Saint Sebastian. My
first child was growing up, more and more often your
father would put aside anything that didn't have to do
with work or with you, and your grandmother's help was
outstanding. But even so, everything was difficult with
you in the beginning, Beñat. You didn't like to breastfeed
and sometimes it felt like you'd rather play with the nipple than nurse. That's why I still remember with a pleasant shiver the bite you gave my nipple when you finally
decided to nurse. Also, it was hard for you to fall asleep,
and for a long time you woke up more than once in the
night. That's why, unlike Miren, you slept in our room
for almost a year.

"Music worked better than anything else to calm your
tears then. I would turn on the radio, to a station that
played classical music, or sometimes I would sing you a
calm song—"The Sea is Foggy," mostly. For a long time
I said everything to you either in song or in verse. I still
remember the verse I would sing you to sleep with and the
one I sang while burping you after you nursed.

"Because of all this, that Christmas your father managed to win what I had denied him in previous years. By
then we had spent several Christmases together and we
both tried to give it the least importance possible. I had
no parents or brothers or sisters, and we spent Christmas
Eve at your grandmother's house almost from the time we
met. Your grandmother took on most of the work and I
found it pleasant how she celebrated the holidays. She put
a little Baby Jesus in the bedroom on the chest of drawers,

and a couple pine branches in the living room, tied with a red or gold ribbon. And that was it.

"That Christmas, however, we spent Christmas Eve at home, with your grandmother but at our house, not at hers, and your father filled the house with decorations. You were too little, Beñat, to notice anything, but your sister was amazed at everything, especially the tree and the flashing lights, as if instead of being at home she were in the middle of a shop. See, said your father, it doesn't cost a thing and the kids will thank us for the effort forever. I didn't really agree; even as a child I didn't like that holiday very much, nor would I later in life. But at that time I didn't know that after a few more Christmases you would disappear, nor do I know now when we will start spending Christmas together again.

"And it seems that the exception, which we agreed to in order not to take you, Beñat, out of the house at an unseasonable time, became a tradition: the following years as well, we had Christmas dinner at our house, each year with more ornaments than the last. Only for few years, however, due to your father's theft of you.

"Before that school year was over, you had started to calm down, Beñat. You woke up at least twice in the night, but you fell asleep more easily than in the beginning, almost without crying. And you, Miren, just then you made your first friends that spring: Olatz and Ane, your true sisters, you said once when Beñat woke you from a deep sleep. I remember that I met your friends' parents and we often got together with some of them or others on the weekends, Sunday afternoons, for example, Beñat in the stroller and you girls playing endlessly.

"I haven't forgotten that your father rarely came with us those afternoons, he stayed at home scowling, and more

e rd Notebook

than once he told me that I was obsessed with always having to meet someone, that we were better off just the four of us, comfy and cozy. But my childhood had been quite lonely and I didn't want that for my children."

There's a break in the notebook at this point, and L doesn't even change her posture when she reads on. She is on the bed, lying face down, with her knees bent and heels in the air.

"The message I received in the middle of that last sentence told me that this evening I will have the chance to deliver this notebook into the hands of the person who will take it to you, today or who knows when. Three days have passed since I received your picture and the note that so upset me, and barely forty-eight hours since I made my request of my messenger to you."

At the end of that sentence, L takes her eyes from the notebook, as if the last words were written in fire. Messenger, Mother wrote, and at that moment they both have aliases, she and Mother. L remembers that the town festival had just finished when Mother received the message, a message that provoked an undeniable crisis. I need you and as soon as possible, right now.

Fortunately, Mother's hiding place wasn't as awkward as other times, and within a few hours the two women met. As soon as she said good afternoon, Mother asked L if there had been any change in her jail sentence and the answer was no. Then she asked what risk she would run if she went to South America without the protection of the organization. L was surprised at the question, but had learned long ago not to show it. She told her she would risk the pending twenty years.

L knew, before Mother even said it, that she liked plain words, straight answers. After she had listened and heard, Mother stayed quiet for a long time, eyes closed at first, and open but unseeing later. When she started talking, she said she had two children, the older one a girl and the second one a boy, that the last seven years had been totally lost for her, that in that time she had received no news whatsoever of them. Their father stole them from me, said Mother slowly and deliberately, and that the night before, she had learned where the children were: in Caracas.

L already knew that Mother had two children; it was on all the papers and even though they had never brought it up, L had always thought that Mother had left her family, not the other way around. While she was thinking this, Mother added that she was writing a long letter, and she needed someone to take what she wrote to the children.

L thought that she hadn't understood, but yes, that was Mother's request: to go to Caracas as soon as possible, get in touch with the children and give the letter to them, without anyone else finding out about it, especially not their father and his new wife. As soon as possible, she stated again, and said that L would have to stay there without feeling rushed, and stay as long as she could.

Once L clearly understood the request, she started thinking about it. Mother told her she would pay for everything, she needed her time and freedom, not money. L asked if it would be too late to answer the next day, she had to check her appointment book. Mother shook her head no and, for the first time since they met, took L's hands in hers. She told her she knew it was a lot to ask, too much undoubtedly, but that for her it was a matter of life or death. L squeezed her hands and Mother immediately let go, as if she thought she had gone too far.

Lighting a cigarette, Mother said that finding the children had changed her life from the roots up; she felt as if she had been let out of jail and from then on, as soon as she understood the new situation, she would dedicate all her effort to getting back together with the children.

It seemed to L that Mother wasn't talking to her, that she was thinking out loud or that her words were directed to someone else. She stood up suddenly and said she had run out of time. She often used that turn of phrase, as if she had been before the court or in jail. L also stood up and had to tell her that perhaps the task was too difficult, that it called not only for time and freedom, but for other abilities as well. Mother silenced her with a gesture from her right hand. She told L that she knew she had made the best choice, that she couldn't be wrong, she had long since lost that luxury.

When L was alone, she felt proud, perhaps because the last words had been said for that purpose. She knew she would go to Caracas, perhaps even the next day, and she would not ask anyone's permission or opinion. It seemed to her that the task had come to her at the perfect moment, just when she was feeling the need to get away, when something inside her was telling her she had to go far away. She immediately saw the benefits of not being able to give details and took advantage of that protection.

"So, few hours remain to me, after so many years. Again and again, when the story seems to become tangled, when I don't know how to continue despite knowing the whole thing by heart, the weight of all my fears enters me through a hidden crevice, all the way in to my heart. I'm not a fearful person, or at least I don't think I am nor do the people around me. But if the report I received tells the truth, that is, that you call your father's wife *mamá*, maybe you have forgotten me or they told you I was dead. Or who knows what? Perhaps there is a glass wall between us as invisible as it is unbreakable and I will try in vain to call you, to reach you.

"As in novels, I can see myself unable to prove that I am your mother. I've had worse thoughts as well. About language, for example. If you have erased Basque together with my memory, this notebook will be as incomprehensible as hieroglyphics to you. My mind has an answer for that as well: in that case my messenger will translate what I've written and then, once the language problem is solved, what I've told you will become a memory for you—not a complete one, I'm not that ambitious, but at least a sliver, a spark, a familiar tune.

"Now I have to return to what I was telling you. It was the beginning of 1981 and you, little Miren, were three years old, and you, Beñat, four months. I started work again in February, on a reduced schedule, after leaving you, Beñat, at your grandmother's house in the morning and you, Miren, at school. Your father didn't want to put Beñat in daycare at so young an age; he said you still needed tender loving care and that you would be better off with your grandmother while I was at work.

"So I only worked in the morning and I had lunch at your grandmother's house every day; we went from there to pick you up, Miren, and then home from there. During that period, I had hardly any meetings or free evenings, since you, Beñat, still weren't staying overnight at your grandmother's. I didn't understand then as well as now the importance of what your grandmother did, but I thought you shouldn't stay there until you were able to sleep the whole night through without waking up.

"In the meantime, you, Miren, were learning your new place, like violets in the forest that flower without causing problems or asking permission. You still had doubts for a couple weeks, the disquiet caused by the newcomer. Later, you decided that you too needed to take care of Beñat, and you would give me a fresh diaper from the box or pick up a fallen t-shirt for me.

"A mother who has not known the hiatus that we have suffered surely would not remember her children's early childhood as well as I do. Perhaps when what happens in later years becomes a memory, other memories get displaced, like how a drop falling into a full bucket pushes out another one.

"Many memories don't always work the way they should, and maybe that's why the memory sent to me now by my archives is from a little later on.

"Summer vacation had just started when you got sick, Beñat. At that time, just at the gateway to vacation, your father often said that you weren't growing like you should, Beñat, you got sick too often, even if the illnesses each time were nothing to worry about. It was colds mostly, I can hardly even remember your face at that time without snot, or hear a cough without automatically remembering your coughing fits. Now you understand, said the pediatrician, why people say 'snot-nosed kids.'

"I wasn't worried or, at least, I wouldn't admit it to myself. Everyone knows that all children are different, and it didn't seem like a very good idea to keep repeating that Miren was easier; it was hard enough for you to learn your place in this world.

"The summer had just started when one night it seemed to us you were almost smothering. It was two o'clock but your father hadn't gone to bed yet. In those days he used to say he was at his best when we were all in bed, his loved ones asleep and he awake, reading most of the time—that was a sign of happiness.

"Your father woke me up telling me we had to go to the hospital. Or that was the first thing I understood, the hospital. I was up when he repeated that you, Beñat, could hardly breathe and indeed, from the crib at my side, deep wheezing reached my ears. We raced into our clothes and your father carried Miren in his arms and I carried you as we ran down the stairs as if escaping from a fire. Your color wasn't bad, but your mouth was open like that of a fish out of water, seeking oxygen. Nevertheless, the air was somehow getting through the dirty sea in your throat, since you weren't turning blue.

"We made almost the whole journey in silence, your father driving the car, Miren asleep at my side, and you in my arms, desperately trying to catch your breath, without giving up, with the same strong will you had before you were born. We're not going to make it, said your father at the bottom of the hill to the clinic, and added that it would be our fault for not going earlier. I thought the same thing, that you could die. The doctors, however, said you would get better, no doubt about it, but that you had to stay there and that we couldn't stay with you at night, or at least not at your side. We left the hospital to take Miren to your grandmother almost without understanding what had happened. We lost no time in returning to the hospital, not to your side, but to be close to you. I'm telling you the truth when I say that your father was angry. Such a hurry to come into this world, he said, and now he doesn't like it."

L's eyes feel heavy, but her feet have started to calm down. It is late and she thinks she has done enough work for the day. An image from Picasso's *Guernica* comes to her: a mother screaming with her son's body in her arms. When she turns out the light, she sees that she didn't close the shades, but she doesn't move. She's asleep by now.

The next day, she gets the car right after breakfast and goes to the CCCT. There, in the shop where she made the business cards, she writes a letter to the parents of the children in gymnastics. The clerks recognize her and L thanks them for the greeting before she sits down at a computer. In half an hour, she has eight identical letters, and she has put them in nice envelopes and written the names, most of which she has never heard before. By noon, she has taken them to the school and has been promised that they will be delivered.

She has three empty days ahead of her. On Saturday, she'll do the same thing she did the week before, go to San Luis early in the morning and wait there, since setting things up with the school doesn't eliminate other possibilities. She goes back to the hotel, but doesn't feel like sitting in her room. The sun has started to toast the city but she goes out anyway, on foot.

She heads up to the hills full of elegant houses. There are more mountains behind them, steeper ones. That's where the poor people live, the needy that are so evident throughout the city, trying to sell something or just begging. One day, she thinks, already protected by the silence of all the elegant neighborhoods in the world, they will all come down to the city together, and they won't come to ask for anything, but to claim what they want. And she likes imagining the people flooding downhill, happy and singing, all colors of the rainbow from black to red, dark-haired and proud.

In the meantime, she's gasping for breath and she sits down on the first bench she sees. She raises her eyes and there in front of her, on a wall that hides who knows what elegance and wealth, she reads a grafitto written in black in Spanish: "Almerinda, you were right, I want to go back," and in place of a signature, a five-pointed star.

I want to go back, back, back, says an echo inside her, but to where? Home, of course, but not just any-one's home. She recognizes that she has no one to return to, unless it's to Mother. What would it be like to live in a city where the graffiti were about love instead of politics, she thinks without envy, and the answer is the countryside by Txingudi, seen from the sea, waves of mountains flowing down the rocks of Aia.

She goes down the hill, the grafitto song turning around and around endlessly in her head. She thinks of the Mexican, and not just because of the song. He is the only person she knows in Caracas, the one who showed her she didn't belong to a couple, but she hasn't felt right ever since she took the lead. Even less so when she remembers the speech he gave her about his children. She seems to be surrounded by children, fenced in, besieged.

"You were in the hospital for six days, Beñat, when you were nine months old and, as soon as my initial fear was over, it seemed to me that we understood each other and that, in your own way, you felt our torment, perhaps more than your own pain. I can say that at the time that you got well, I observed, like never before, that you were happy with us, as if the solitude of the hospital had shown you the value of what you had.

"In the meantime, you, Miren, were with your grandmother in Gros, close to the beach you liked so much. Summer or winter, you and your grandmother went to the beach, from the time you were very little, even in the rain. I remember after spending the whole day with Beñat in the hospital, I went to your grandmother's in the afternoon to pick you up. It was raining: large, warm drops. It was eight o'clock in the evening, but you weren't home. Without hesitating, I went around the corner to the beach. Right there, against the jetty, I saw two shadows, one small and red, the other bigger and dark blue. There you were, trying to catch crabs, and it seemed to me that paradise must look something like that. The sea was your obsession; you always said Gros beach when I asked you where you wanted to go. Grandma's beach, you said, to Grandma's beach.

"The summer that started so badly ended well. As soon as you got home, Beñat, you blossomed, as if the curiosity that was so characteristic of you even before you were born had increased with your illness. Before you were one year old you learned to walk and you spent the whole day going back and forth like an ant. On the street as well, in your stroller, you looked from one side to the other without wasting a second, as if your job were to supervise. You got mad, first quietly, but soon shouting, if I stopped the stroller for two seconds.

"I remember once, that same summer, a few days after you got out of the hospital, we were walking on the Concha beach, you in your stroller and me pushing it, and your cap fell on the ground or at least that's what I thought. I leaned over, picked up your hat, put it back on you, centered on your head, and set off again. Two steps later I saw as clear as day that you were taking off your hat and throwing it to the ground yourself. I picked the hat up again and with my face right in front of yours told you that you didn't know who you were dealing with, that there was no use throwing your damned cap to the ground again, it was sunny and you needed it. That's what we did for the next five minutes, you throwing it down and me picking it up without saying a word, you smiling and me getting angrier and angrier.

"You won finally, like most of the competitions that were to follow. In that also the two of you were so different, from birth itself, by nature, not because of your family or your surroundings. I don't think it was an accident of gender, but that's philosophy. Some day, who knows when, we'll sit beside each other telling stories, something we can discuss if we ever have time for small talk. And we will, we'll make it happen."

SIX

Before falling asleep, she wasn't sure which feeling prevailed about the weekend. On the one hand, she thought that she should take the opportunity to see a bit of Venezuela: the forest, the Indians, the very proximity of the tropics.

She knows she won't make much progress if she stays there—the report has been set in motion—but she doesn't want to go too far from the children, as if the net cast by Mother had caught her. So she wakes up adrift, thoughts scattered to the four winds.

The ring of the telephone wakes her all the way up, and before she answers it she thinks it must be the Mexican. An unfamiliar voice greets her and then tells her that downstairs at the reception desk there is an urgent letter for her. From the Mexican, she thinks.

She stands up, takes her pants from the back of a chair and has only just put them on when someone knocks at the door. She opens the door, takes the letter, thanks the messenger and, after putting the letter on the little table, lies down on the bed without taking off her pants. She has another quarter of an hour before the alarm goes off, but she's awake now and can't do anything about it.

She gets up and goes into the bathroom without reading the letter, but before she gets under the shower, she goes back to the room to turn on the television. There is news on two or three channels, sports on the rest of them. So many options, but she can't find any music and there is no radio in the room.

She goes down to the hotel café for breakfast and there, waiting for her order to come, she reads the letter. This evening, at seven o'clock, on Sabana Grande Boulevard, on the terrace of the Golden Café. She reads it twice, and then goes on, even though she hasn't really understood the message. Come, says the letter next, I have a gift for you. And a capital letter M as a signature. Nothing more. The whole letter is typed.

As she drinks her coffee, the words fall into place: the M must mean Mother, without a doubt. The person who gave her the task, however, has a real name as well as a number of less real ones, as L well knows. Those names don't begin with M, but L doesn't doubt who it must be.

This is what L has: if she starts to think about it, if she really concentrates, she knows that lightning finds the best route through the air, the path of least resistance. She decides to go spy on the children and there, while she is waiting, she will have a long time to scrutinize the letter.

The highways aren't as crowded as before, or perhaps she knows the way better now. The sun is high, as if it were there to stay. I will fry, she thinks as she starts up the hill to San Luis. The neighborhood seems to be sleeping and it doesn't even occur to her that the people she has to spy on may be gone.

She doesn't park in the same place as last week but on the sidewalk across the street. She doesn't want a repeat performance with the dog, and she is sure that it won't happen, especially since she has good reason to stay awake. After taking a sip of the cold cola she brought from the hotel café, she reads the letter again even though she almost knows it by heart. She thinks that if it wasn't written by Mother, she has reason to be afraid, but she can't imagine who, other than Mother, could want to speak with her and have the opportunity to do so. Especially the opportunity, since she didn't tell anyone she was coming to Caracas, and her parents wouldn't have received the postcards she sent them yet.

She looks for Sabana Grande on the Caracas map and finds it quickly, not very far from the hotel, maybe even close enough to walk. She decides to keep spying until about five o'clock in the afternoon, be at the hotel by six and at the appointed place at the appointed time. Then she tears the letter into tiny pieces and puts them into the empty cola can.

As time goes on, there starts to be a little movement on the street. By now she is regretting not having finished the notebook the night before; perhaps it would have shed more light on the situation. She examines for the millionth time everything that she has done since coming to Caracas and thinks that before going to her meeting she should call the Mexican so that he doesn't back out of the report. Fanning herself with the colorful supplement to the newspaper she hasn't read yet, she tries to cool the heat that is beading her forehead in sweat.

By noon, she's pouring sweat and has starting thinking perhaps it would be worth it to go back to the hotel earlier to finish the notebook before her meeting. Suppose Mother is the one who wants to quit and has ordered the person who wrote the letter to get the notebook back. L is not getting anywhere like this, but her desire to finish the notebook doesn't let up.

It's about half past noon when she sees the father, the girl and the dog coming out of the building. They go down the hill, just as they did the week before. I've already seen this movie, L thinks, and keeps watching, looking at the point where the trio disappeared. Barely ten minutes later, the group returns. The girl comes back looking down at the ground and the father is talking, waving his arms. They don't seem angry, but what the father is saying is certainly not without emotion.

In the next half hour the street empties again, and L thinks that she's suffering the heat for nothing; the children won't come out until the sun goes down and by then she has to be at the hotel. So she starts the motor and is heartily grateful for the cool breeze that blows into the car as she goes down the hill, even though it isn't much.

As soon as she gets back to her room, she showers and, without having any lunch, picks up the notebook and begins to read.

"When the school year began, I happily took up the normal rhythm of the year again. You started going to daycare, Beñat, again against your grandmother's will. You were one year old, and Miren was four. I was a bit out of practice, since the previous year I had worked only in the morning. Furthermore, for the first time in a long time they gave me the older kids to teach and that made my work more difficult. But I did it happily.

"Your father used to say I didn't know how to sit still and do nothing, and he must have been right, since at that time I was always running from one thing to the next. Yes, I have always liked action more than contemplation.

"It is true that in addition to family and work, I had a few other worries, and so did your father. We had met each other under certain conditions, and under those conditions we had endured more than ten years. I hadn't changed, but maybe your father had. I say maybe because at the time he still showed no sign of it.

"So I had less time to be with you, while your father, on the other hand, had more and more. But this situation didn't cause any tension between us or, to be more exact, if it did, I didn't notice it. I thought we were a team, the four of us and your grandmother, a team well adapted to each other.

"So I started work and even though that would be the last school year of my life, there was still no indication of it. That's the delightful thing about life: there's no warning of what will happen. Maybe right now, maybe I have only a few months left in which to hug you, but I still don't know. Even just a week ago I didn't know what you're like today.

"Talking about your appearance, it occurs to me that maybe I should send you a picture of myself, but people like me don't take pictures, or at least not happily. Besides, I'd rather have you read what I'm writing first. Then it will be time for pictures and it calms me down to think this, that we have a future, that is. In these seven years, as you have gained, so have I lost. I was a young girl when they stole you from me but for a while now, I have been a grown woman, one of those women who is proud not to be called young.

"That school year, though, immediately got complicated, in all senses, in all areas; I don't know why. You, Beñat, had at last learned to sleep through the night without waking up, but you were often sick. Nothing serious, fortunately, but your throat, lungs, and ears were always ready to welcome any germ in the area. At the time I used to say that if a germ didn't come close enough, you yourself would catch it in your hands. Miren too learned very quickly to give you nose drops and soon all of us, the whole family, including your grandmother, were specialists, more so than some pediatricians.

"Fortunately, so many medicines and fevers didn't take away your appetite and in addition to what was prepared for you, you would take anything off our plates, cod and even endives from the salad. Your grandmother used to say she was happy to work long hours in the kitchen just to see how much you appreciated it. You liked everything, you wanted to try everything, and this behavior made you, Miren, a little jealous, perhaps because Beñat won our admiration with it. You see, my darling, I would say that after seeing Beñat eating beef stew when he was two, you also had to taste it, but you were very stubborn and sometimes I was also a pain in the neck: come on, honey, just a little bite, you don't know what you're missing, and so on. Depending on your mood, you would give in or else close your mouth and get mad, saying that your grandmother's chicken tasted better or that my croquettes were dry. But that happened rarely; normally mealtimes were not a problem in our house because I'm a reasonably good cook or I was, and all of us, your father first and foremost, liked to eat well."

L stops her reading and closes her eyes with the notebook still in her hands. Hunger and memory merge, and in a rush she sees again the dinners and the evenings that she spent with Mother. In fact, a cookbook was the first gift Mother ever gave her. Tasting foreign foods was supposedly the easiest way to travel for people in her situation. That's how Mother begins or ends a lot of sentences— "people like me" or "people in my situation"—using the plural because there's safety in numbers. From the very beginning, however, it has seemed to L that Mother was a wholly special woman and not only because she lived sur-rounded by men and the men treated her as if she were a normal and complete person. Mother was also a woman without family and that seemed a miracle to L.

Before putting away the notebook, L looks to see how many pages are left. At a glance, she sees that she still has a number of pages to go and that on the last ones, Mother's handwriting goes downhill a bit. She is hungry and she decides that she should eat something in order to better face the afternoon. In order not to waste time, she chooses the hotel café, even though the Chinese restaurant across the street is tempting. Besides, snacktime is more impor-tant in Caracas than lunchtime.

She chooses a vegetarian sandwich and a very cold Coke. In the meantime, she decides how she will dress and how she will fix her hair and make-up. Her thoughts tangle up on her and finally lead to the Mexican and, as soon as she pays for her lunch, she calls him. No, the man isn't in, so she leaves a message for him to call her in the evening, please.

As soon as she enters her room she takes a new t-shirt out of the dresser, and the high-heeled shoes and a tight skirt, the color of the sky over Jaizkibel mountain at dusk, that she normally wears with a t-shirt or big sweater. She goes into the bathroom, wets her hair and returns with a big white towel wrapped around her head, puts the skirt to one side and puts the black pants in its place. Then, she throws the towel to the floor and puts lots of gel in her hair, emphasizing her natural curls. This is one advantage of the hotel: they give her clean towels every day.

Sitting in the armchair in the corner, she begins to read the notebook again, head up, waiting for her hair to dry. It will turn out best that way, if it dries by itself, curliest.

"I didn't measure my strength well, no, nor the enemy's either. And now, now suddenly I have to add the most difficult point. I have an hour or an hour remains to me, if I want to take advantage of today's opportunity. So, after all the delay because of all my fears, I will launch into what they did to us like someone jumping headfirst into the cold ocean.

"February had just begun and it seemed that winter would last forever among us, as if the earth had forgotten the way to the sun. I was home alone with a cold or something. You two were at school, your father was in Madrid in one of those courses he used to take every now and then. It was the middle of the morning when I got the news and even though I was in bed, I followed orders without hesitation. I was out the door in a minute, with the hood of my anorak up, bag over my shoulder. And I never returned.

"I crossed the street and then went through the park in the rain. I called your grandmother from a phone booth by the side of the road. I might be late, I said, and before I asked her for anything she told me she would pick you up from school. She also asked if I was okay, and I didn't quite understand what she was talking about. As soon as I had received the order, I completely forgot about my cold.

"You were five years old, Miren, and you, Beñat, were two. At the time, I didn't do such calculations, I thought it would be a matter of a few hours, that I would be home in time for bed.

"But that's not how it turned out. I had to go away and your father agreed. He gave me nothing but protection once he had hurried back from Madrid. I was in the French Basque Country, of course, safe from our enemies, and that's what he told me, to keep calm, the children were fine, your grandmother sent a big kiss and besides, things would soon settle down and then the four of us would go on vacation, seeking the sun, to forget the rough times. I cried on his shoulder for the first time since I got the order. No, he said, I shouldn't cry, it wouldn't be for long, and as soon as I gave the okay he would bring the children to whatever place I told him.

"I've already said that that winter seemed to last forever, but it didn't; when I saw you again in a couple weeks, it was spring in the sky and on the ground. Hardly two weeks had passed and, changing with the season, you had gotten bigger, older. You, Miren, had your hair pulled back the way I liked it, and there was no trace of snot on your face, Beñat, until you started to cry.

"They gave us a house for two days and one night and even though the place was strange to all of us, we fell into our usual attitudes, all four of us, as soon as we got together, as if it were a winter Sunday afternoon. You asked me why I didn't come home, Miren, and your father twisted his mouth, as if he had told you in advance not to mention that. I explained to you that a bad policeman was after me, but that he couldn't catch me. The explanation didn't please your father, I saw it immediately in his glance, but he let me continue.

"You told me you wanted to stay with me and you wouldn't be any trouble at all. I'll take care of you, you said, and I didn't take it as a joke. Believe it or not, and it's certainly not the most appropriate feeling, but almost from the time you were born, I felt more like you were taking care of me than like I was taking care of you. I didn't know how to answer and, in the absence of words, opened my arms to you. While we were hugging, your father said that he had to go away, he couldn't stay with us, I don't remember why. Later I often wondered why your father couldn't stay with us those days, and if he really left or did I censor his image? I can find no answer, but I am telling my version of the story, my truth; lies will be accidents that happen against my will.

"The house had a nice kitchen, like the one that must still be in your grandmother's house, and we were there for a long time, making dinner for the three of us, chatting, telling stories, until we made the room our own. Then after dinner, we showered and went right to bed. It was cool outside the kitchen and besides, Beñat's eyes were closing. There was a room with two beds, but you, Miren, immediately said we would sleep better all three of us together in the big bed. That's what we did and as we were getting into bed, it occurred to me that I should ask your father for some sheets from home for just such occasions.

"You didn't want to go to sleep, Miren, but you, Beñat, fell asleep like never before, out cold all of a sudden on the edge of the bed, with your thumb in your mouth. Miren and I started talking, telling each other stories. In the opinion of your teachers, if you were ahead of your peers in one thing, it would be talking. That evening, covers pulled up to our chins in the haven of the reddish light on the night table, the game we would later call Theater was born. We weren't ourselves, but others. That first time, I was a mother bear and you were a bear cub, a mother and daughter never separated for any reason.

"The bear cub fell asleep at some point and before turning out the light I thought that through our theater you had shown me what you had hidden. In a low voice

I told you, both of you, that I would soon be home, certainly before the school year ended.

"Then I went around the bed to your side, Beñat. I took your thumb out of your mouth and took you into my arms, as I could no longer do with Miren. You were very hot under your pajamas, but you didn't seem to have a fever, no, just the warmth that was needed to make my hug more tender. Perhaps heat is the feeling that is strongest for me. I gave you a kiss and felt a hot ball between your nose and your chin. I have often thought that that might be the soul, or life, or love, that sweet heat that I have never known since. After I lost you, I never wanted to touch another child. I looked at them, I asked their age and tried to imagine what you would be like, but without touching them.

"The next morning we were wolves and Beñat also took part, but not for long. You tired of a game quickly, within a few minutes, and then did something else, always seeking something new. You would pick up any toy or anything, it would seem like there was nothing better on earth, and you'd drop it a few minutes later to pick up a second or third toy.

"So you and I, Miren, played a whole bestiary together. I was always the mother and you were always the child, the little child, often a newborn. But that only happened when we were playing Theater; otherwise, Miren, you liked to play the bigger one, the grown-up.

"It seemed I couldn't go home, and the weeks went by slowly for me. Your father told me I shouldn't be in such a hurry, that it wasn't only me who was at risk, we would see what happened after the summer was over, he and the children would soon be on vacation. I don't remember word for word what we talked about in those conversations, but I do remember the messages your father sent me, or at least the ones I knew about. I've gone back over things a million times trying to find out if he sent me any warning before he took you and disappeared into thin air, but I've never found anything.

"Before the summer, we had become acquainted with many other houses, and sometimes your father too stayed with us. Never did more than two weeks pass without my being with you, and at the end of the school year you spent four days with me.

"Then came the day in the pine forest, the end of a week the four of us had spent camping. In that vacation, Miren, you had brought a chain that you wore around your neck, a gift from your grandmother. Hanging from the chain was a silver charm with a lid and everything. And under the lid, there I was, smiling, cut out of a photo of our group they had taken against my will."

At that point L puts down the notebook on the little table at her side and closes her eyes. She thinks that she's very similar to Beñat when he was little, she often wants to change activities, wants to go from flower to flower, as her father would say; a child who will never reach adulthood, in the words of her alleged boyfriend. She knows that she has only a few pages to go to finish the notebook and she thinks that before the final push, she should move a little, her body cries out for it.

She stands up, looks out through the half lowered blinds to the traffic below. After making sure in the mirror that her hair is drying well, she looks at the chair waiting for her in the corner by the window. The clock tells her not to waste time.

Finally, she picks up the notebook and lies on her stomach on the bed.

"It came time for you to go home and for me to return to a place with no name. Your father and I made plans for the next weekend, just the two of us, without kids, he said, so that we wouldn't forget that we were also a couple. It wouldn't be the end of the world. By then my sadness, the pain I felt in being away from you, had begun to seem normal. Two weeks seemed a bit too much to me, but I agreed to your father's plan.

"And you melted into space with no warning, while I was away from home and on the run. Your father didn't come like he promised, and at first I thought there must have been a problem, something with the police or maybe an illness. I was disappointed but not at all worried. I just had to wait seven more days, that's all.

"However, I soon had to accept that the problem that had come up was impossible for me to solve: you and your father had disappeared, even your grandmother had no news of you. Or that's what she told me, in an elegantly written letter. My son stole them from us, she wrote, and said that as soon as she found anything out, she would send me a note.

"Seven years later your father sent her a Christmas card from Venezuela. In the meantime, everything went through my mind as I sought the roots of this void that looked like it would go on forever. You were dead, all three of you, your father had killed you, I don't know. Perhaps the only hypothesis I didn't examine was the right one.

"During those years I often imagined that I put a message in a bottle and that the sea would carry it to you; at least to you, Miren—if anything remains to you of your childhood, it would be the sea. I threw hundreds of imaginary bottles into the water without throwing in a single real one. Then I sometimes thought that my message had reached a long, hot beach and was waiting there for you. Other times, I thought the glass had broken to bits against the rocks and my message had been lost in the water.

"They will come back to me, I pray many times a day like a Buddhist, when they're older, they'll come back to me. I've never lost hope completely. Believe it or not, I can honestly say that that kept me alive: more than once, I wanted to die, but even in my darkest moments, I thought I couldn't die like that, without knowing where you were, the scraps of my life had to strengthen and nourish your lives; I couldn't just disappear into nothingness.

"And here I am, even if I don't know exactly where, as much on the run as I was when your father kidnapped you, but not forever. It will take a long time to play out because it's not easy to change the orbit of a satellite, but from now on my life has no other purpose.

"Memory by memory, I have told you my little piece of the truth. Now you know who you were and that I will always be waiting for you. In the absence of anything else, I would like to die at your side, like a tree whose leaves serve to enrich the ground around it. Not, however, before hugging you, before tasting your smell and your heat at least one more time.

"See you soon, my darlings, my sweethearts. Until we see each other, leave me a trail, mark your path for me. The person who brings you this notebook will tell you how.

Mother."

Contrary to what L expected, her eyes don't fill with tears when she finishes the notebook. This deep suffering has put her mind to sleep, or perhaps it was the voice that orders her to go to the children and to hug them like Mother wants to. Of course she doesn't do that. For a little while she rests her face on the sheets without worrying about her curls. Then she gets up and gets dressed without hurrying. Before she leaves the room she hides the red notebook behind the dresser.

She goes on foot to the designated café, map in hand, light rope-soled sandals on her feet and the new shoes in her bag. It is hot, but the breeze makes it more bearable.

The first kilometer, starting across the street from the hotel, is under a highway. There, in the sky, at least ten stories above, the sound of motors is a distant thunder. It is half past six and she hardly sees anybody on the street, which is not yet completely constructed.

The highway takes a sudden turn to the right and down. The street, however, keeps going straight and the sun hurts her eyes. By now, she knows who might be behind the letter she received. Excluding the police and people like that, she thinks Mother must be behind everything, either willingly or by chance.

Ever since she left the darkness under the highway behind, the street has slowly started to deserve the title. She has it clear in her mind how to behave, and feels no fear, just a gentle nervousness. While she walks on, she looks in the windows of the houses, as she often does. How many lives there are right beside us and we'll never know most of them, Mother said to her once when they were walking together down the street.

She thinks she should change her shoes soon, she can't do it in front of the café, but she doesn't feel up to walking far in those miserable things. When the street starts to fill up with shops, she takes off the rope-soled sandals, like her cousins from the farm used to do when they went into town for mass when she was little. She notices that she's looking at the asphalt from farther away now and that she carries her body straighter. In a mirror offered by a clothing store, she looks to make sure that her curls fall where they should. It is ten minutes to seven when she thinks she should ask where the Golden Café is. But she sees it before she asks, almost at the farthest point of her vision, a reddish neon light saying Golden in capital letters.

The hour has not yet struck when L sits down near the middle of the left side of the terrace. The table has a flowery parasol wide open over it, in orange, and the other people on the terrace have also chosen tables with parasols. The waiter comes over as soon as she sits down, but she has decided in advance what to order. She asks for an iced coffee and sits attentively, waiting, looking around, stroking her hair from top to bottom with her open right hand, slowly, as if her hair were made of fragile crystal. We need a little music, she thinks, as if she were in a movie. It is hot in the shade too, but she doesn't feel damp with sweat.

They bring her the coffee and make her pay the bill; she is putting her wallet into her bag when someone sits down beside her. Good afternoon, he says in Basque, and before she answers, says that they will have to speak in Spanish from now on. L turns her head as if in no hurry, and as soon as her eyes find the source of the voice, the man falls quiet. He is not young, he must be fifty or so, and his body has gone spherical, with neither neck nor waist. If it weren't for his shirt, she would say he was on a terrace in Biarritz or San Sebastian. Okay, says L, and waits again.

While the waiter brings the man a rum punch, they do not speak. Then the man says he has to give her a letter. L realizes she's pretending to be calm but isn't. Calm comes to her once she knows why the man called her here. The ice has completely melted in her coffee, but it's still cool. The man says if she lets it sit, it will be warm in ten minutes, and L asks him how they will transfer the letter.

The rum punch doesn't have time to get warm. The man says they will get up together and he will pass her the envelope when they are surrounded by people. He is sweating, but he doesn't seem to realize it. When L again looks straight ahead, the man asks her if she has anything for the person who sent the letter, any message. L needs to tell him it's too late for that, she will return in a week, but keeps quiet in time. No, she says, no message, just tell her everything is going well.

The man says they will get up and head to the right. They do and are immediately surrounded by people. Then the fat man, moving smoothly, gives L a thick envelope from the jacket he carries in his hands and she immediately puts it in her bag. A few steps later, the man stretches out his hand to her and disappears down a street to the left. L stays there for a few seconds, standing in the middle of the beehive of activity. The damned sandals are hurting her feet and she would like to run away.

It is eight o'clock when a taxi drops her off in front of the hotel. She hasn't changed her shoes and every step makes her heels burn. She is carrying her bag under her arm and has the impression that she is dangling from it as she moves forward. She is a few steps from the reception desk when she hears someone calling her name from behind her. Without turning her head, she recognizes the Mexican and, before turning around, takes off her shoes.

The Mexican wants to go out for dinner and L's instinct warns her that she can't say no: she has to secure the report at school the next day and without that, she has nothing. She asks for ten minutes to go to her room and change clothes. The man answers by sitting down in an armchair and spreading his hands wide.

As she enters the room, she throws her sandals to the floor, and puts her hand in her purse as soon as she sets it down on the bed. There is the envelope, full of words. She knows she doesn't have much time, and quickly rips off the paper. Inside, another envelope, quite thick, and a letter in Mother's hand. It is only two pages long and L doesn't want to read them. She puts everything in the hiding place with the notebook finally and gets into the shower, almost racing. Only two pages, she repeats under her breath.

She goes out of the room and while she's waiting for the elevator it occurs to her that maybe Mother wants to back out, maybe that's what she says in the letter, not to give the notebook to the children. But then why the fat envelope that came with the letter? And she returns to the room. She feels that she has to read the letter, even if it will double the promised ten minutes.

My loyal friend, says the heading. Even though I hurriedly wrote the notebook in your hands, I think I remember every word in it. I could repeat all of it right now, word for word. That's why I'm sending you this envelope, to expand on what I said there. Please tell them it would be better if they read what I'm sending you now first, before beginning the notebook, like a prologue.

She stops reading there, as soon as she has made sure that Mother doesn't want to back out. She hides the notebook again and, before going out, stands before the mirror. She fluffs up her hair a little and goes down to the Mexican with her bag over her shoulder.

When they go outside, the sky has gone purple in the west. The man doesn't object when she says she's very tired, nor when she tells him that she wants to return as soon as possible. They go into the Chinese restaurant across the street and as soon as they sit down, L brings up Monday. The man has his answer at the ready: as soon as he knows the children at school have permission, he will call the office and everything will be ready for Tuesday. Everything is clear, L says to herself, but the knot in her stomach that she got when she opened Mother's letter doesn't loosen. She swallows the food she ordered with difficulty, as if she were already full.

To escape her unease, she asks the man about his family, his children, and the man takes the bait. From then on, L is on automatic pilot and the Mexican's voice drifts away from her, recedes. She thinks she acted like a child when she found out that there were only two pages for her and at least ten for the children. She doesn't admit to herself that the knot in her stomach is curiosity.

Suddenly the man falls quiet, not only to swallow a bite or drink some beer. Actually, it is the length of the pause that rouses her sleeping attention. She doesn't know exactly what he was talking about before he went quiet and L makes use of one of those handy all-purpose phrases. The man says you shouldn't trust people who don't love children, they are not generous people, they discriminate. First they keep children out, he says, then old people, then the handicapped, and it gets worse from there. Children are people, not little animals. He is not joking, but the Mexican's face has its smile like his speech has its music. L says she's exhausted, she's had a very long day, and the man immediately holds up his hand. Our Basque men are going to look even worse to you if you get used to this, she warns herself.

It is half past ten when she enters her hotel room and by then her plea of exhaustion has come true. She takes off the clothes she's wearing, puts on a loose white t-shirt and retrieves the letter from the afternoon. She starts reading standing up, beginning with the second paragraph.

"Ever since you left, I feel that my future is in your hands and, because it is a feeling as familiar as it is unpleasant, I repeat to myself many times a day that I couldn't be in better hands.

"Please, be careful when you get in touch with the children, be careful with the father who stole them and be careful, especially careful, with them, they may have forgotten me or been told I was dead. Use with them the instinct you have always used with me and the words will come to you on their own. Explain to them how I live and what I'm fighting for, tell them that you yourself will help me find them, that I won't lose them a second time, that the thief should worry.

"Better yet, don't tell them the thief should worry or anything bad about their father, in case it frightens them. Find them and give them the notebook and with it the prologue I'm sending you."

At this point, when she still has a whole page of the letter yet to read, L stops reading. From where she is, she can see the other envelope on the bed, white and thick. She thinks she could open it and then buy another envelope, there's nothing special about this one. She even imagines herself opening the letter in the steam of the electrical gadget she sometimes uses to make coffee. After shaking her head hard, she continues reading.

"And don't forget I want photos, if possible taken from closer up than the one you have. Do all this, my dear friend, and come back soon, come back as soon as possible. As the saint said, I live without living inside myself, waiting to hear from you.

"I must close this note without saying thank you because thanks are too meager to repay the debt I will owe you forever."

L folds the pages carefully and leaves them on the little table with the other envelope. She doesn't tear open the new envelope, even though her curiosity nearly robs her of sleep.

SEVEN

She wakes up early in the morning, as soon as the sun enters her room and, taking advantage of the impetus this gives her, she goes out almost by the time the children are in school. On the way, which she knows by heart by now, she reviews her next steps: what she should say to the secretary or the Mother Superior and how to arrange for the report. While she parks, it occurs to her that she made the journey almost without thinking about it, as if she had gone from her village to San Sebastian. She has always liked cars, from her father's big Renault to the Ford she now has waiting in front of her house. She has always found driving pleasant and even relaxing. She gets into a car, into the driver's seat, and turns on the motor and the music at the same time. Then the highway, hands always on the wheel, and whole body on automatic pilot.

With this trivia on her mind, she goes up the stairs in the sun, which is not too hot yet. When she reaches the top of the stairs, she sees that the big entrance door is closed. She doesn't sense any danger, however. The small door in the middle of the big door is open and she enters that way. Then, as soon as she crosses the threshold, she hears a deep and total silence, the kind that makes your heart twinge. Without understanding what's going on, she goes into the office, and there's only one person there. No, the secretary isn't home, nor will she be until the holiday is over. She says "home" meaning the school and then mentions a holiday.

L feels a lightning bolt right through her body, as if the fluorescent light had dropped on her from the ceiling. Yes, they have three days of vacation: Monday, Tuesday and Wednesday. What's more, the unknown woman doesn't know anything about the report, nobody told her anything.

L sits down at the top of the stairs, head in her hands, dumbfounded and feeling more lost than when her suitcase hadn't appeared at the airport. At first she thinks that her two weeks of work have been for nothing, she's done nothing but waste her time. Soon she stands up and runs down the stairs even though she doesn't know where she's going or what she's doing. As she gets into the car, she can hardly hold in the tears, and the Mexican is the only salvation she can think of. She knows the man can't change the holiday, but she needs to believe that someone will help her. Sitting there before starting the motor, it occurs to her that the children will be back on Thursday and she still has until Friday to do the report. She gets out of the car and calls the Mexican. He isn't in his office, but he'll be back soon. She leaves him a message that she'll call him that night at his hotel.

She puts the car in gear and heads for San Luis, toward the neighborhood where the children live. She parks where she was spying the night before and spends long hours there, anxiously. The sun is at its hottest when she gets out of the car and goes down the hill. If she doesn't drink something, she'll never last there—that's why she dares to get out of the car. Anyway, even if she runs into the children, she has her hair pulled back at the nape of her neck and that calms her down.

She asks for a very cold cola in the first bar she finds, and it occurs to her with the first gulp that perhaps the children aren't in Caracas; maybe they went away for the holiday. Now that she thinks about it, it immediately occurs to her that this would explain the night before; perhaps they left that weekend. By the time she returns to the car, the theory seems better than it did at first and, with the notebook she always carries in her purse and a felt-tip pen, she tries to find a solution. In vain, however.

It must be about five o'clock when it occurs to her to go to Macuto. She has always preferred doing something to sitting around waiting, so she doesn't ponder Macuto for very long. She immediately starts the motor and soon she is on the highway that goes to the airport. Sunset is not far off when she gets to Macuto, and she goes right to the outskirts of town to the north.

Neither the old van nor any other car is in front of the gate of the house that is so familiar by now. She leaves the car around the curve a little farther down the road, as she did the first time, the right side of the car almost in the brambles. She approaches the house she wants to spy on as if she were simply going for a walk. Bushes she didn't notice when she was there before cover half the fence with red flowers. No voices or other noises come from inside.

She thinks she should return to the hotel, but doesn't. Instead, she goes down to the sea, which is the color of lead, the knot in her stomach unrelenting. She doesn't see anyone around but even so, she doesn't allow the imminent tears to flow, and roughly wipes from her face the few that break through her eyelashes. She sits down where the sand begins, with her knees bent and her head resting on them. She gradually starts to feel better, but hates how tearful she's been since she has been in Caracas. The sky is purple over the sea and from time to time she hears birds that are not gulls calling, nothing else.

She stands up, picks up her shoes and goes to the edge of the water until she feels the sea, which is as warm as the air. Then she gathers up her longish skirt and walks a little bit along the shore toward the south, moving like an old woman. A few yards further on, a tongue of land covered with plants blocks her way. Nice metaphor, she thinks as she returns to the north. Her ideas won't come clearly, she sees no way out.

It'll be dark soon, she thinks, and in front of her, several yards from where she is, she sees a bump on the sand, close to the water. As she goes closer, she sees that it's a person, and after a few more steps it seems to be a young girl. L's interior fog is too thick to let in this ray of light.

Only a few steps remain from where she is to the person on the sand, who then raises her head from her knees. Suddenly, L finds her eyes locked with Mother's. No, it's not Mother, she understands immediately, but the girl.

Somehow she keeps moving forward, eyes to the north. This is your big chance, she thinks, now or never. But she doesn't know what to say or how to approach the girl. Use with them the instinct you have always used with me, she remembers, and hears another voice saying that the trick lies in knowing how to take advantage of the opportunity. It seems longer to L, but only a few minutes have passed since she saw the girl when she turns back toward the south. The girl is still there, in the same place and position. Neither the father nor anyone else is around, and over the sea the first stars have come out.

She can't find the words and there are only four or five yards left before she reaches the girl. She walks forward with her eyes on the sand, body full of adrenaline. She sees out of the corner of her eye that the girl is standing up and she wants to stop, but is ashamed of the feeling.

"She sent you, didn't she?" she hears in Spanish when she has not quite reached the girl. She doesn't have to raise her eyes to know who is talking. She meets Mother's gaze again and stops with her mouth open, like a fish out of water. "I know she sent you," the girl says, and L nods her head yes.

"Mire-e-en," they hear from above, no doubt from the door of the house. It's a woman's voice and the girl heads back toward dry land, seeking the shelter of the bushes. The girl yells back that she's coming. Then, looking at L, says that she'll be there the next day at six o'clock in the afternoon, and goes off through the brambles. From there, she answers L that, no, she hasn't forgotten her Basque completely. And she runs up the hill until she is lost in the sky, which is not yet completely dark.

L sits down right there, or falls to the ground, exhausted, like the little shepherds after seeing the Virgin Mother. She thinks she must be dreaming, or is stuck in a South American novel. But no. The girl noticed her, maybe saw her before at the door of the school or at San Luis. "I know she sent you"—that's what the girl said, word for word, and her voice, no, her voice is not like Mother's, and won't be as deep as Mother's when she's grown up either.

The night is now completely black, and on the way up the hill L gets scratches on her arms and legs. The light over the door is on at the girl's house, and a little music drifts out to the highway; it must be a harp. When L gets into the car, she thinks maybe it's not worth it to return to Caracas if she has to come back the next day. She starts the motor, turns around in the same place as before, and thinks maybe there's a hotel in Macuto. She immediately discards the idea, as soon as she remembers that tomorrow she has to bring the notebook and the last letter. She puts on her seatbelt and heads for the highway, debating whether or not to call the Mexican. She has always been talkative, almost loquacious, and even though she thought she had it under control, her experience in Caracas has shown her that talking is essential for her, as essential as eating. She regrets not having brought cassettes from home, and looks for and finds music on the radio, classical, baroque, but she doesn't know the composer.

It is late when she reaches the hotel, at least ten o'clock. She definitely wants to discuss what happened with someone, and the Mexican is her only option. So without going up to her room, she calls the Mexican from the phone by the entrance. Besides, that's what she had arranged to do in the morning. The man is in his room and answers after two rings. He asks L if she's had dinner yet and they arrange to go out for dinner at the bar where they met since it's close by for both of them and, besides, it's not that easy to get dinner in Caracas at that hour.

She doesn't feel like changing her clothes or going up to her room. Before going out, she gives in to an impulse and asks at the reception desk if she has any messages. She hardly knows the receptionist, it's the night shift. After looking a few places, the man says no, no messages for her. With a sigh she heads for the elevator out of habit, but turns around in front of the armed man, who always seems to be the same person, and goes outside.

She is thinking about Mother's gaze and the girl's, every face on her way to the bar makes her think about it, that gaze that shows neither doubt nor surprise. What happened seems unbelievable and she doesn't know how much she can tell the Mexican. As she crosses the park, she feels the first breath of censorship: it seems to her that Mother would not approve of her behavior, it wouldn't seem graceful to her. No, Mother won't care about her methods, only her results.

The park is quiet, deserted, and she can clearly hear the hum of the breeze that has started to bring the temperature down. Seen from there, the bar with its brazen neon light seems too noisy, and she almost regrets having called the Mexican. Besides, she has neither the desire nor the energy to hear Chavela Vargas. It occurs to her that it would have the same effect if she wrote what happened, but it's too late now.

The man is at the door. His greeting does her good and she shows it. He asks if she has good news or bad and then, right away, if he has to wake up early the next day. Since the news is good, they each order a rum punch at the bar. The man asks for her watch and, to banish the surprised look he gets as an answer, adds that he'll give it back to her at the hotel. L obeys.

The Mexican is talkative too, but he is also a good listener. L tells him that the client who sent her to Caracas lost her children seven years ago and that her job is to get in touch with those children. She doesn't say why Mother can't do the job herself, but does explain how the children live and with whom. Then she tells him what happened that day, starting at the school and ending at the beach. She tells the last part in great detail, as if she wants to make sure she has everything recorded in her memory.

When they sit down in the small dining room at the back of the bar, the man asks if she's noticed how low the music is. Then when the waiters put enough food in front of each of them to feed ten starving people, the man says he doesn't understand why she's not deliriously happy, since she has successfully completed her task.

L explains that she is happy, but that things came together more by chance than she would have liked. She didn't do things as well as she should have, even if the results were good. But she is happy or, to be precise, touched. The man says that chance is worth nothing if you don't take advantage of opportunities. Before they begin eating, they know they will never clean their plates.

For a long time, the Mexican explains, there's been one little thing he doesn't understand about what happened to L: he doesn't know what constitutes motherhood. L doesn't agree with his reasoning; she says hands-on experience is not the only way. The man sticks to his guns and soon, with the ice cream, he talks about his children. L doesn't care what direction the conversation takes, it seems to her that it's the Mexican's turn.

It is almost two o'clock when the two of them set off for L's hotel. The Mexican says it's no time to be on the street alone and walking together doesn't seem like a bad idea to L. The man says he'll be waiting the next evening at his hotel, so she can call him at any hour. As they turn the corner to the hotel, L thanks him for the time he's wasted with her. The man silences her with a gesture. He's the one who should thank L and, under the light of the hotel, he takes her right hand and kisses it. Then, almost without touching her wrist, he puts her watch back on. Before he leaves, he asks her to be careful, and L nods her head yes, and waves goodbye, good night, with the hand he kissed.

Ten minutes later she is asleep, the notebook and addendum under the pillow on the side of the bed she isn't using. Before she fell asleep she tried a trick she uses from time to time, one that she learned in order to have the dreams she wants. Most of the time it doesn't work, maybe because she doesn't try hard enough, but this North American Indian system has worked for her several times. You have to fall asleep thinking about your hands and then, when you start dreaming, you have to move them. That's how the Indians are supposed to have opened the door to their dreams and L tries it because she would like to get in touch with Mother, she would like to tell Mother what happened. She concentrates on her hands but, finally, just before she falls asleep, she is thinking about Mother, not her hands.

She wakes up very early the next day and even though she searches her mind at the very first second, she can't remember any of her dreams. It is eight o'clock, but it feels as if she slept for twenty-four hours. She thinks about the girl, even before thinking of Mother. She sees her on the beach, sitting down, looking at the sea, and she remembers the red raincoat, Gros beach.

She leaps up and goes out after putting on the first clothes that come to hand. She wants to have breakfast and be outside. She turns left from the hotel without having decided what nearby café to have breakfast in. She sits down at the first one that looks authentic, in the shade of an incredible ficus tree. She orders papaya juice and a chicken *arepa* with coffee. For the first time since she's been in Caracas, she feels like she's on vacation. Even more than the food, seeing indoor plants outside is a sure sign of being abroad.

The thick ficus leaves are unrivaled for blocking the sun and, while she has breakfast, the coolness she feels stays with her, there in the shade of the tree. She wants to find a stationery store to wrap up the notebook and the last letter. She knows she won't open the letter, even though her curiosity of the day before yesterday has not lessened. She wouldn't betray Mother like that, nor anyone else. It was a bit of a stretch even to read the notebook, though it turned out to be useful to her later. When she saw that the school was closed, when she thought she had lost the children, she didn't remember immediately about the red raincoat, but something led her from San Luis to Macuto.

Before finding a stationery store, she finds a shopping area she hadn't known about on the same street as the hotel. There, on the lower floor, she finds a bookstore. First she looks at folders the size of the notebook, but she doesn't find any she likes and can't guess which Mother would have chosen. She thinks Mother would have chosen something for little kids, since she must surely still be thinking of the children she lost, not the ones in the photograph, not the ones L knows. Finally, she chooses a plain brown envelope, thinking that it will place more importance on its contents.

She buys the envelope and heads back to the hotel. She's not in a hurry, she has the whole morning to get ready for the afternoon. The Mexican comes to mind when she sees the armed man at the door, and she feels proud on the whole, but doesn't take the trouble to examine why.

When she enters the room, she sees that the maid hasn't come yet, and that annoys her a little. She thought to review the notebook, but starts to pick up the clothes scattered to all corners of the room. When she's almost finished, the maid comes in and L goes down to the lobby because she has always felt embarrassed when someone is cleaning up around her, embarrassment and the need to help the person cleaning. She spends the next quarter of an hour skimming the newspaper, just the headlines. She doesn't find anything about the Basque Country in the international news.

When she goes back up to the room, everything is tidy in a sort of shining dirtiness, but like her mother used to say, if the bed is made, the house is clean. Before opening the notebook, she turns the envelope over in her hands three or four times as if there were something to see from the outside. Then she starts on the notebook from the very beginning.

As if she were seeing a movie she'd already seen, the second reading shows her new angles, unknown stars. She is lying on her stomach on the bed, with her head resting on her hands and the black notebook on her right. From time to time, she writes a note in it, that she needs to take photos or to ask the girl about her Basque again first thing. As if she were at work.

By noon, she has filled two pages with notes, on each line a dash followed by two or three words. She takes a break and goes to the window. She would like to see the sea, but she knows she will see the foggy glass of an office building. The language is the first thing she has to clarify—what did the girl mean when she said she hadn't forgotten her Basque completely? Then she'll tell her about Mother's situation and that's the hardest part. Your mother is fighting for the Basque Country, or your mother is a freedom fighter. She doesn't think those are the right words, but nothing else comes to mind at the moment, or at least not sentences that are appropriate to what happened on the beach. Without having reached a decision, she picks up the red notebook again, this time sitting in the armchair by the window. She has taken off her pants, but even so has started to feel the heat. She will have to turn on the air conditioner soon.

When lunchtime arrives, she's not very hungry. She feels like her belly is full of words. She takes a break anyway, to help her find the words she has to say to the girl, her own words, not Mother's or García Márquez's. After looking at the clock, she decides to eat something at the hotel, then take a short half-hour break and then it will be time to get ready for Macuto.

She drives to the beach almost automatically, trying to settle on what she has to tell the girl. She feels like she's gotten the hang of the traffic. She has chosen her clothes carefully: she is dressed in dark blue from head to toe, and wears her hair down. It is five o'clock when she reaches Macuto and, at the edge of the water, the sun is half hidden in cloud, unlike in Caracas.

She leaves the car quite a bit farther away than before, in a safer place. When she approaches the house, she hears faraway voices from the beach, laughter and shouts. She goes down the hill carefully, afraid of running into the family face to face. And yes, there are the children and the stepmother, another woman, and two smaller children playing in their midst. She doesn't see the father, but he may be there; she doesn't look for him for long. She wants to find a good hiding place and, in order to find one, has to sit down on the ground among the brambles, which have neither fruit nor flowers.

At least an hour later, the sound of the voices changes. Straightening up a little, she sees that the group is getting ready to go, and it looks like the girl is carrying her little brother in her arms. From her hiding place, L hears lots of sounds as they go up the hill, and a man's cough. The father, she thinks, even though he could belong to the other family.

It is a quarter past six when the area is quiet, and L stays put, afraid that the girl won't show up. Then she straightens up and sees no one on the beach. She goes down to the water, almost leaping because of the hill. Her feet feel like they are in tatters and she soaks them in the warm, still water with her shoes in her hands. From there she looks toward the house and sees no movement. She can't believe the girl won't come; it seems to her she could easily come up out of the sea or drop from the heavy clouds above.

She comes down the hill, however, dressed in white, almost flying. She stops where the sand becomes smooth and signals from rather far away. She points to the north and L heads that way at a good clip, behind the girl. There is no noise other than the low murmur of the sea and the calls of the birds.

Where the embankment turns sharply to the left, L loses sight of the girl, but she immediately sees her again, right there, smiling, Mother herself as a young girl. When L stops in front of her, they look at each other and without saying a word, the girl sits down on the ground among the brambles. L does the same, clutching her bag to her breast.

She's dying to ask how the girl guessed that Mother sent her. She asks about the girl's Basque first, following her plan, and the girl answers that since they left home they hardly ever speak Basque, just a few words sprinkled in here and there. It's obvious that the girl isn't very concerned about the language issue; something else is bothering her. She asks L why Mother sent her, and L puts her hand in her bag and says that inside the envelope there is a notebook, without mentioning that it's written in Basque. The girl asks where Mother is, not where and what she's doing, not why she's not with them.

Looking at the sea, L begins to speak, deliberately, word by word. She tells the girl that she will learn the answers by reading the notebook, but that above all else, she has to keep something in mind: Mother didn't leave them, their father left Mother. Then she explains that Mother didn't know where her children were for seven years, or even if they were still alive, until she got the news from Venezuela a short time ago. The girl listens carefully and when L falls silent, takes a pendant from under her jacket, silver, oval. Inside it, under a picture of her little brother, Mother appears, in the photo clipping mentioned in the notebook, colors faded with time.

L says that Mother and her daughter are very similar in body and in looks, and that now Mother is quite a bit thinner than in the photo. She wants to tell her about the Basque language, but the girl gets in ahead of her. She says they went to Mexico first, the father and the two children, and that from the beginning he told them their mother was dead, but that she never believed it, and never let Beñat believe it. She has always known they would find each other again, inevitably, and not in heaven. The girl's speech is lovely, with the Venezuelan lilt. Bit by bit, she fits her little brother's picture back over Mother's face and replaces the charm on her bosom.

The sun is hidden behind the peak of the farthest mountain and the girl says that they don't have much time. Then she reaches out her hand for the notebook. L repeats that it's written in Basque and she won't understand it, and that she herself won't be able to help, because she's going back to the Basque Country in a few days.

The girl doesn't pull back the hand she reached out and answers that she doesn't care, she will learn it by heart until she understands what is hidden in the words. Just like Mother, thinks L, and says that if the girl wants, she will translate what Mother wrote. The girl doesn't answer right away, but drops her outstretched hand before mentioning that they will return to Caracas the next day. When L tells her about the report, the girl offers her a startled smile, the first sign that she's surprised, and then says her father didn't give permission in the end. Finally, without the girl's agreeing to the translation, they arrange to meet Thursday morning at nine o'clock, just inside the main entrance to the school. It's a safe place, she says, since neither her father nor his wife ever go up the stairs with them. Her father and his wife, she says, without using the word *mother*.

After making sure the appointment is clear, the girl stands up and L asks her to stay a little longer. She sits down again and L explains why Mother herself didn't come to give them the notebook, that she's fighting for the freedom of the Basque Country and cannot move freely about the world. The girl asks if that's why she left home, and L vigorously confirms the idea, in words, nodding, with her whole body, over and over. Then she says the girl will understand everything better once she reads the notebook.

With this, the girl stands up again and so does L. She asks the girl how they live, how she gets on with her father and his wife. The girl first answers by shrugging her shoulders. Then she says they get along well, but that it doesn't matter, matters even less now that she knows that Mother is alive.

Then, after already taking a few steps toward the house, she says to tell her mother they're okay and that in a few years, as soon as she's eighteen, she'll go looking for her and she'll find her no matter where she is.

L doesn't want to let the girl go. She would like to give her the hug Mother would have given her, but she doesn't have the nerve, it doesn't seem appropriate. Instead, she says why doesn't the girl write Mother a letter, and the girl leaves, waving her hand, without saying yes or no. L says that she has to give her one more message, that Mother wants photos, needs them, and the girl says she'll bring some, she won't forget. Then she goes as quickly as she arrived. After going around the outcrop of land, L sees a white speck among the brambles, heading uphill against the sky, which by now has started to get dark. "Mire-e-en," she hears, and a faint voice barely carried on the wind that could be the father's.

The beach is dark and there are no stars in the sky, but L doesn't move away from there. On the contrary, she goes back and after sitting down in the hiding place she used with the girl, she writes in the black notebook points that will help her remember the conversation well. Mother dead, Mexico, Basque translation, father, eighteen years old. With her pen in her mouth, she searches her memory looking for more. As soon as she turns eighteen, she writes, she will find her, no matter where she is.

There is only light traffic on her way back to the city, and L arrives at the hotel quite a bit earlier than the night before. However, she doesn't call the Mexican. She goes straight to the café and there, while eating a completely tasteless sandwich to calm her insides, she completes the notes she took on the beach without forgetting a single word.

As soon as she goes up to her room, she calls the Mexican and gives him a summary of what happened. They don't arrange to meet that evening because L wants to start translating the notebook into Spanish immediately. The man doesn't object and they agree to talk the next day. She likes the man and likes the relationship they have even more.

Before starting anything, L tidies the room as if she were organizing her mind at the same time. The job doesn't take long, and the table is cleared off. Then she goes over to the lamp beside the armchair and turns it on. When everything seems as it should to her, she takes the brown envelope out of her bag and sets it on the middle of the table. She showers and puts on a clean t-shirt—of the ones she brought to sleep in, the only one she hasn't worn. She is ready.

She doesn't worry for long about not having a computer, and sets to work willingly. She takes the pages that she's written on out of her black notebook and starts on the pages that remain. "I am your mother . . . " She writes carefully but quickly, as if she were used to the work of translating and to some extent she is, but most often translates from Spanish into Basque. When she finishes the first paragraph, she lifts her felt-tip pen and checks to see how what she has written looks. Mother's handwriting is sharper, and quite a bit larger.

As she goes on, she gets stuck on a sentence more and more frequently, and not because she has trouble translating. The substance gets confused, the meaning; and when that happens, she always remembers some event or, worse, a memory that contradicts her image of Mother, as if Mother had been unknown to her before she read the notebook.

It's late, no doubt about it, even though she has forgotten the clock in the bathroom. She must have translated about a quarter of it, and she decides that's enough.
She would rather wake up early tomorrow than work
until late. She would happily drink a cola—when she
closes the notebooks and stands up, she suffers a sudden
thirst—but her first thought in response to this craving is
money, the need to save. However, it immediately occurs
to her that she won't have to pay for the report, and then
she feels rich.

So she dresses in the clothes she wore to Macuto and
goes down to the street with her bag over her shoulder. It
is two o'clock in the morning and the hotel street is a dark
desert. She hasn't got the courage to go on, or rather, it
doesn't seem wise. She returns and asks for a cold caffeine-
free cola at the reception desk. They'll bring it up to her
right away, says the receptionist, and while he's writing
down her order, he asks her if she wants the cola plain,
without gin. Yes, just like that, plain, as cold as possible
but without ice, especially no ice.

That night, without L's doing anything to control her
dreams, Mother comes to her, looking for the children. L
tells her they are not children, the girl has been a young
woman for a while now and the boy is already a young
man; she will have to raise her arms now, not lower them,
stretch out her legs, not bend her knees. The two friends
are in a wide, green field, behind a house that cannot be
seen. From where they are no roads or paths can be seen,
but both have their eyes on the horizon of the field in
front of them. The sun makes its journey in that direction, and when it's about to go down, Mother says that
while she's waiting, she'll take a nap, and she falls asleep

right there, in the field, curled up, a blood-red poppy in the green wheat.

That's as much as L remembers of the dream when she wakes up, even though she knows it went on. For at least five minutes, she stays in bed in the position she was in when she woke up, without moving anything. Hopeless, the rest of the dream is lost in the synapses of her brain and she will certainly never find it again, or it will pop up unexpectedly.

She leaps up, throws her t-shirt and underpants to the floor and gets into the shower for a long time, head under the water. Then, dressed in the clothes from the night before, she has breakfast in the hotel. By nine o'clock she's working on the translation again. She starts without reading what came before, because she knows if she starts correcting what she's translated, she'll never finish.

She has about half of it, maybe a little more, in Spanish when she takes a break. The boy was just born. So she has finished the part that makes her the most uneasy and she wants to go out. She is about to leave when she thinks she ought to translate the addendum as well and she puts the unopened envelope in her bag before going to the café she went to the night before.

There are too many people under the ficus tree and, since the terrace continues to the left, she crosses the café and goes to the far end of it. That's where the patio ends, among the gardenias. She orders two large *arepas*, one hot and one cold. Giving in to a last-minute impulse, she changes her order, first a rum punch, then the *arepas*, she tells the black waiter.

With the first gulp, recent memories come rushing back to her: the Mexican, Chavela Vargas, the girl on the beach, the frangipani in front of the school. Nevertheless, without delay she opens the envelope and begins to read the handwriting that by now is as familiar to her as her own.

"My dear children, Beñat and Miren, Miren and Beñat. I am your mother, that is what I want to tell you. I am your mother and I am alive, because among other reasons I could not die until I see you again.

"I am your mother and I love you, inescapably, more than I love myself. That's how things are now, in these seven years I have spent far away from you, and that's how things were before, when your father stole you. For that is what happened: your father kidnapped you, unexpectedly and secretly.

"You are my daughter and my son and, before your father decided otherwise, it seemed to me that you were pieces of my body, that you and I could not live apart from each other.

"Obviously I was wrong: according to the only photograph I have managed to get, you grew and got bigger far away from me; without me you became who you are today, and here am I, a wilting plant that for too long has not known the sweet sun."

L cuts off her reading at this point, mad as hell. She doesn't like Mother's tone, she thinks she's playing the victim. For her and for many other people, Mother is a person of great renown, a woman of wide authority, not the helpless bird of the addendum. L knows that the person who wrote the notebook is not the person she thought she knew. But "wilting plant" is an exaggeration, pure self-pity. She is tempted to change a few things as she translates, but leaves the decision for later.

"So you have been without me longer than you were with me and, furthermore, I don't know what your father has told you, with what information he hid your flight, his theft. More to the point, I have no proof of what I'm saying, not even a single photograph.

"Your memories are my only salvation, especially yours, Miren, because you were six years old when your father separated us. Perhaps when I least expect it, on the weakest page of the notebook, something will tell you, yes, you experienced that and it was stored there in a corner of your mind, safe from your father's grasp."

L raises her eyes and rests them on the white flowers on her left. She's translating, she has to repeat to herself, not spying through the keyhole. The rum punch is reddish, not pink, in the light of day, but it tastes just like evening.

"So read what I've written and don't forget that I'm waiting for you, forever. Waiting, that is my sin and the behavior I have to change, starting now. I can tell you that when I had to leave home, I didn't know what sort of hole I was falling into, and had I known, I would have chosen jail. If I had chosen that path, we would have been together by now, but it's too late now to change what has happened.

"I wanted to change society, make a better world, belong to a free country. Your father wanted the same things, but that's another story. Because I wanted to achieve those goals, I set off, meeting by meeting, step by step, into exile. And long before I achieved anything, I harmed my family, and I harmed my son and daughter, whom I love better than anything or anyone else.

"I didn't think about that then, of course, but that doesn't change anything. At the end of a few months I was left with nothing: no children, no husband, no home. The only thing I can offer as an excuse is that I was devastated, I couldn't understand what had happened, I was trapped in a nightmare.

"And I didn't wake up until I found out that you were in Caracas, but even so, I was still in exile. After you disappeared I had, once, the chance to return home, but by then I had no home and no family, and I didn't take advantage of the opportunity."

L stops reading right there, folds the pages and puts them back in their envelope. She doesn't want to keep reading or can't; both probably. She feels rage first, then pity. She thinks that if Mother were at her side, she would shake her to wake her up. She signals the waiter that it's time for the *arepas* and, while the food is coming from the kitchen to the table, considers not translating the addendum.

When she's back in the room working, the Mexican calls and they arrange to meet that evening at nine, at the bar which by now is the usual place. As soon as she hangs up the phone, she concentrates on the task in hand and writes for a long time, without stopping, without opinions, as if she were an automatic translating machine. Because of this, she still has an hour before her meeting when she finishes the translation. The notebook, that is; the addendum she leaves until evening.

When she stands up, she feels her exhaustion, the knot in her back that is almost a pain, and she resists the temptation to lie down on the bed. If I lie down, she reasons, I'll fall asleep. After sniffing her armpits, she decides she'd better take a shower, so she does. Then, wasting no time, she gets dressed and goes out. Without realizing it, she carries the addendum in her bag, though she hid the two notebooks in their usual place behind the dresser. She's wearing jeans and gym shoes.

On her way to the bar, she thinks it will be hard for her to return to her usual life; she will never forget the weeks she's spent in Caracas. With the exception of Mother, all the people close to her have disappeared from her memory, even the one she thought was her boyfriend, and the thought of returning home almost makes her afraid, as if she had to return to an unknown place.

The wind, which until then had been pleasant, is annoying as she crosses the park, but there are no clouds in sight. She thinks about the girl, who should be in Caracas by now, and about various sentences that she read in the addendum, the most painful ones, in fact.

The man arrives wanting to talk and L happily falls into conversation because, after so many emotions, she has arrived at some sort of tranquility. He speaks to her of Venezuela, and suggests a walk on Friday. Apparently, she can't leave without feeling a hint of the jungle; it would be a sin to see only Caracas and Macuto.

While they are eating dinner, the Mexican asks after Mother, and L adds more detail to what she told him the night before, but without mentioning the latest letter. She says she has finished translating the notebook and the next morning she will give what she has written to the girl. The man immediately senses that she doesn't want to talk about it and returns to the initial conversation. L doesn't finish what she ordered and the Mexican eats everything she left on her plate.

It's not yet midnight when she returns to the hotel and she doesn't make the same choice as the night before. She sets the alarm for five o'clock in the morning and is asleep on the bed before she knows it.

As soon as she wakes up, she drinks an approximation of coffee made with hot water from the bathroom and sits at the table, seeking the concentration she had the night before. She knows the addendum will be harder for her than the notebook, and not only because the writing is less familiar to her. Nevertheless, she arrives at the end of the part she had read without getting too tired. She needs a break in order to be able to continue, and she picks up her scattered clothes. Then curiosity wins over fear and she continues translating.

She is unable to recapture the atmosphere of the night before and stumbles forward, against her will in many sentences. In this mood she writes out Mother's painful self-criticism, but the clock forbids her to go slowly, and a quiet voice forbids her to lie. Granted, when a word suggests two translations, she chooses the softer one, always the one more apt for the person she knew before reading the notebook.

"I was crushed," Mother wrote, "I gave up, and that is what I can never forgive myself for, even though it is hard for me to accept it, that's what hurt you as much as your father's behavior." For L, however, if there is anyone in this world who has never given in, it would be Mother.

When she finishes the translation, she decides to leave without having breakfast because she doesn't have a lot of time. Because of this, she arrives at the school half an hour earlier than necessary. There in the car, which is not yet frying in the sun, she considers for the last time the possibility of giving the girl only the notebook and its translation. Finally, she puts all the papers into the envelope and puts the envelope in her bag. She waits beside her old friend the frangipani, watching the cars that stop at the entrance. If she starts walking as soon as she sees the van, she'll be able to go up the stairs right after the girl and won't have to wait inside the school.

It's five minutes to nine and even though the van hasn't come into view, she crosses the street and, as soon as she climbs to the first level, she sees the black heap, last in line. She goes up the stairs as calmly as possible and feels rather than sees the girl coming up behind her. As soon as she crosses the threshold, she turns left and when she turns around by the wall, there is the girl, alone. By way of a greeting, she says she was afraid L wouldn't come, and L confesses that she felt the same.

L puts her right hand into her bag, grabs the brown envelope, and then leaves it there when the girl holds out a plain white envelope to her. There are pictures in the envelope, the girl says, and she doesn't need the translation, she wants the notebook written by her mother. L wants to say she can have both of them, the notebook and the translation, but the look in the girl's eyes stops her. The girl adds that she doesn't want any intermediary, she will learn to understand her mother's voice, no matter what.

L doesn't want to hear what the girl is saying. She tells the girl she won't understand anything, she asks her, please, to take the translation even if she doesn't want to read it right now. L doesn't like the light in the girl's eyes, but she doesn't have time to think about it. The girl doesn't give in, she shakes her head no and holds out her hand for the notebook, more like Mother than ever.

L takes the brown envelope out of her bag with her right hand, tears it open at the fold and holds out the red notebook to the girl. At the same time, she says that the next day she would like to give the girl a letter she herself wrote on her own, at the same time and place, if that's okay. The girl doesn't answer right away, and L says she would like to tell her what she knows about Mother, she wants to tell her that Mother isn't just anybody, that everyone who knows her loves her, and that more than that, she is a much admired woman.

Just then a jarring bell rings and before obeying it, the girl shakes her head no. She doesn't need explanations, the notebook is enough, and she thanks L for doing her job as a messenger so well. She repeats that as soon as she's eighteen, she'll go look for her.

There are still latecomers at the entrance, but it's clear that the girl has to go. Indeed, she tucks the notebook into her bosom, under the white shirt, and has taken a couple steps when L asks her for one last minute. She would like to hug her, she says, and the girl looks startled, but doesn't stop L from hugging her. A few seconds and, almost running, she is lost down the long hall.

Hondarribia, 1996–1998